LOX & CREAM CHEESE

Eric Stromsvold

Worpswede Press
New York, NY

All contents in this book are a work of fiction. Characters, scenes and dialogue are solely products of the author's imagination and should not to be construed as real. However, some real life locations are used for purposes of creating a reality within the story.

Worpswede Press
New York, NY

ISBN-13: 978-0-6159291-0-1

For John T. Tubman, in memoriam.

Chapter 1

The scent of old lady perfume is lingering in the air of the bank. It continues to waft through the air where a too young to be wearing it woman once stood a minute ago. The inappropriately perfumed young woman is now standing at the front of the line and waiting for the next teller. Billy stands three people behind this young woman. He is wearing sunglasses, a bucket hat, round Band-Aid bandages on all of his fingertips, and a fake nose and cleft chin that he stole from a prop house several months ago. He casually breathes in the old lady perfume as the yellow fluorescent lighting above flickers from a power surge. Billy finds the scent of the perfume to be relaxing. He is about to rob the bank and needs to remain calm, so he is welcoming the perfume scent in the air. Staying calm is what will help Billy get away with the robbery. He always does his best to blend in with everyone on the line right up until the moment he slips the teller a note stating that he is there to rob the bank. Nobody will notice that a thing is amiss until Billy is at the bulletproof glass. Even then, only the teller will know that something is awry. Everyone else in the bank tends to be too busy wondering what their long wait is for. Once Billy's cover is blown, he will only have 15 seconds before he has to be on his way out the door with the cash. Robbing banks is a tricky business and having the entire robbery done as swiftly as possible is the key to getting away with it. Billy's 15-second rule is what has helped him get away with seven bank robberies in the previous two months. The idea to hold up banks took hold in Billy's mind once he began drinking again. He had been on the wagon for a little over eight years at the time when he fell off of it.

The teller, Nancy, smiles and waves Billy over to her commercial transaction window. Billy smiles crookedly at Nancy. As he wishes Nancy a good afternoon, he slips his note beneath the bulletproof glass. Billy holds it there. It reads: BANK ROBBERY! GIVE ME THE LAST FOUR CASH DEPOSITS OR I'M COMING TO YOUR HOUSE MRS. JACOBSON. Nancy's jaw drops with wonder as to how any customer, let alone a bank robber, could possibly know her last name. Both of her name tags only state "Nancy." She begins to perspire as if she is being cooked alive inside of Death Valley on a hot day. Billy lets go of his note and it zips quickly back to his belt. Billy always keeps all of his robbery notes laminated and attached to a retractable key chain on his belt so that he never leaves notes behind as evidence. He knows that bank tellers are trained to drop their robbery notes to the floor to save the notes as evidence for the responding authorities.

Billy always asks for the previous cash deposits since there is never a chance of GPS tracking bugs or ink packs being hidden inside of them. Nancy nervously slides the previous four cash deposits beneath the bulletproof glass towards Billy's anxiously awaiting fingers. The deposits are neatly held together in the rubber bands that the previous depositors wrapped them in. Billy places the four bundles of cash into his man-purse, thanks Nancy, and then casually walks out of the bank onto Madison Avenue at the corner of 48th Street as his heart races a mile a minute. The warm and bright midday sun of summer hits Billy's face from a reflection on an office tower as his black leather shoes make tapping sounds along the sidewalk. The reflection of the warm sun feels perfect on Billy's face. He walks hurriedly north for two storefronts before turning back to see if he is being followed. He sees that there is nothing but the normal flow of pedestrians on Madison Avenue behind him. Billy realizes that he is in the clear, so he turns right onto 49th Street and hails a taxi. It will still be several minutes before the police show up to the bank from the silent alarm that Nancy instinctively activated.

Billy tells the taxi driver to take him to Union Square. As he is driven downtown, Billy takes his disguise off, but still leaves the bandages on his fingertips. Billy never wants to leave fingerprints. As he places the cleft chin into his man-purse, Billy smells the cash and smiles and feels relaxed at the scent of old lady perfume that he finds coming out from the bag. Billy pays for the taxi with cash consisting of low denominations from his pocket. He walks through the crowded Union Square farmers market and goes down into the subway.

Billy boards an uptown 6 local train, feels his man-purse and estimates that he has roughly thirty thousand dollars inside of it. Now that Billy is on subway, he feels safe about leaving fingerprints, so he begins to take off the bandages from his fingertips. Thirty grand is a good haul for an hour long lunch break. Billy exits the train at 59th Street and once again blends into the crowds of midtown. After he finishes walking up the staircases from the subway, he buys himself two hotdogs with mustard on them and a can of Diet Coke from a guy with a food cart on the sidewalk. Billy devours the hotdogs and gulps down his soda. This is Billy's favorite quick fix lunch after holding up a bank.

The walk to his office building on Park Avenue is freeing, since Billy knows that he just got away with yet another robbery. Billy quietly enters the building, scans his identification card at the gate in the lobby and gets onto an elevator. Billy exits the elevator at the 43rd floor and walks towards his desk along the carpeted hallways that are eerily quiet. Billy is now Bill, the always punctual employee who is held in high regard by both his peers and boss. None of Billy's coworkers are the wiser of what Billy has done on his lunch break. Billy places the cash filled man-purse into his desk's overhead compartment, logs back into his desktop and closes out the intranet window containing information from the bank's employee database. The page displaying Nancy Jacobson's information disappears from the screen. Billy goes about the rest of his work day as the bank's best anti-money laundering analyst and files several suspicious activity reports on bank clients who have recently deposited large volumes of cash. It is work that Billy finds to be mind-numbingly boring, but it's also work that helps him gather intelligence on which teller in Manhattan normally has large amounts of untraceable cash in their drawer during his lunch hour. Billy spends the rest of his workday the same way that he spends most of his workdays, with his eyes glazed over on autopilot, filing report after report, moving through accounts at a marathoner's pace, all the while, either daydreaming about his young ladyfriend, Mia, or daydreaming about robbing another bank.

Chapter 2

It is late evening. Billy is at home in his one bedroom apartment way out in Brooklyn at the end of the R subway line. The apartment is dimly lit and mostly furnished with second hand furniture and paintings Billy rescued from the trash and flea markets. The apartment smells like only a bachelor lives there and is also filled with far too many houseplants. Billy is sitting on his couch with his two cats curled up next to him. The felines purr with content as Billy looks at his coffee table covered with cash. The lunchtime high that he got from the bank robbery has subsided. He has just finished spending 45 minutes counting and recounting his haul. Altogether Billy's holdup this afternoon has netted him $34,287. It's the second largest heist that Billy has gotten away with and it's all cash that Billy doesn't need at the moment. Billy is still flush with the money from his first bank robbery and also has a six-figure salary from his job at the bank. Billy lives a low cost life. He doesn't own a car or have anything too fancy at his apartment aside from a 60-inch television. Aside from rent, Billy's biggest monthly expenses are his 401K deposits and his affinity for sushi dinner. He has been holding up banks not because he needs or wants cash, but because he enjoys the thrill of it all and the high that the robberies give him.

Billy neatly collects and stacks all of the money from the coffee table. He flips through it and breathes in the scent of old lady perfume once again. Billy places the cash and his prosthetics in a shoebox, covers the cash with several old socks and then carefully places the shoebox beneath the floorboards of his bedroom closet. There is now approximately a quarter million dollars in untraceable cash in Billy's hiding place. Though Billy just had a successful robbery today, he is already looking forward to getting another high from robbing a bank sometime soon, because the high from the robberies is that addictive.

The doorbell rings. It's Mia, Billy's main girl, though he has others because Mia is afraid of commitment and refuses to label Billy as her boyfriend. To Mia, Billy is merely a stretch of roadway on the highway of love. Mia wants to be able to take an exit ramp at any given minute without regret and is okay with Billy seeing other women as long as he doesn't rub it in her face. Mia views the status of this open relationship as making her a true modern woman who is ahead of the curve. Plus, to Mia, Billy's other women take the pressure of commitment and of settling down off of her. Mia stresses about settling down and always feels anxious about the thought of becoming a responsible adult. She feels as though being in a committed relationship makes her one step closer to old age and death, even though she is eight years younger than Billy and is a mere 21 years of age.

Billy opens the door and finds Mia standing in the hallway of his apartment building. She is glowing with beauty, in skin tight black pants, and a pink cut off shirt that reveals her tanned pierced belly button and smooth abs. She also has a paperboy hat on that allows her short curly black hair to bounce out next to her head. Mia's natural Latin tan glistens perfectly in the light of the hallway. Billy's smile lights up at the sight of Mia, as he wishes that she would want to be his only girl. He feels guilty about womanizing when Mia's eyes aren't looking, but knows that things between Mia and himself will likely not work out long term, since Mia is so young and is still trying to figure out who she is. The small blue nose ring on Mia's face is the biggest clue that she is still struggling to find herself. Both Mia and Billy lunge at one another for a hug and a kiss. They are near complete opposites who have managed to fit perfectly together for the past eight months despite the fact that Mia hates the fact that Billy works at the bank. She would probably love to learn that Billy holds up banks but knows nothing of them. While Billy on the other hand hates the fact that Mia is deathly afraid of statues, so much so that she needs to close her eyes in order to walk past them ever since she fainted from fright at the sight of a large three quarter length bust of President Madison.

"I brought you a gift." Mia gleefully tells Billy, as his arms are wrapped around her hips and they drift back and forth in his doorway.

Billy invites Mia inside of his apartment and she sits on the couch. As Billy goes into the kitchen to get glasses of water and a couple of beers, he notices that the scent of old lady perfume is stronger than he thought it was, as it still lingers in the air of his apartment. Mia sits and silently wonders if Billy is sleeping with a geriatric behind her back and is reminded of the time that she went home with a 60-something-year-old bartender. Mia gives herself the shivers and grosses herself out, both from the thought of Billy sleeping with an old lady and her memory of the hairy old Irishman bartender. Mia feels as though she could easily vomit from these thoughts.

Mia hands Billy the present when he returns with the drinks. He takes his time while unwrapping the paper and slowly peels the tape off of the box. Billy wants to save the wrapping paper and reuse it. Mia cannot wait for Billy to open the box and is too excited to see Billy's reaction on what she has come to believe is the perfect gift for the perfect man.

"Come on. Open it already." Mia says, as she rips the box open and pulls her bubble wrapped gift out of the box. "It's a watering can. Do you love it?" Mia's smile is beaming and is making her natural glow even more irresistible. Billy is slightly confused by the watering can but tells Mia that the watering can is beautiful and that he loves it. "Now you don't have to use that old ketchup bottle to water your houseplants. When I saw this watering can I knew that it was the perfect thing for you."

Billy doesn't have the heart to tell Mia that he uses the old ketchup bottle to water his houseplants because he always overwaters his plants whenever he has used a watering can in the past. He has used the same old ketchup bottle for seven years, knows the measurements for each potted plant like the back of his hand and assumes that he will have to pretend to water his plants with this unwanted watering can for the foreseeable future so as to not hurt Mia's feelings. Billy sits and silently wonders how much professional mime classes will cost him to teach him how to effectively pretend to water plants with an empty watering can. Mia grabs Billy's face. They kiss and begin to make love. Afterwards they take a cab out to the bar that Mia works at as a bartender and Billy gets blackout drunk. Several hours later, after they return back to Billy's apartment, they have blackout sex with one another that neither of them remembers having come the morning.

Chapter 3

Billy's office is nearly empty of all of his coworkers as he sits in his cubicle and pretends to keep working into the night. His boss Chris is under the impression that Billy is staying late to finish a report instead of attending the company Christmas party. Billy hasn't been doing any official bank work for over an hour and is actually spending his time scoping out his next potential target. He reads one of his coworkers suspicious activity reports and discovers that a commercial banking teller, Mandi Whalen, at the branch on Park Avenue South at 23rd Street, has been getting a steady cash-heavy deposit midday Monday for the past eleven weeks. Frank Derico makes low five figure deposits most days, but each Monday he goes to Mandi Whalen's teller window at approximately 1:30PM and has been depositing between $40,000 and $50,000 in non-sequential 50s and 100s. Billy suspects that Derico is swapping out smaller bills for the larger ones used in illegal dealings and that Derico is too stupid to realize how suspicious $40,000 in large bills looks to both banks and the government.

   A quick internet search of Frank Derico reveals that he is a club promoter originally from Manhasset, Long Island, who now lives in a spacious apartment around the corner from the bank where he has been making the large cash deposits. Derico is like many other club promoters and club owners in the city in that he is too cheap to hire an armored truck to make his deposits. Instead, Derico chooses to have the club's security goons drive him back to his apartment at 6AM and then makes the deposit himself in the early afternoon after sleeping through the morning.

There are plenty of images of Derico in Billy's internet search. Frank Derico is overly muscular, overly tan, has his eyebrows too manicured to the point they mimic the stay at home moms of Long Island, and is almost always photographed wearing a cheap looking shiny suit guidos from Long Island fall over backwards for because they think it is a high class look. The women Derico is photographed with are the female versions of himself, except they tend to have manlier faces than regular women because they hit the gym too hard and are several inches to a foot taller than Derico. Billy suspects Derico is at best five feet tall and it makes his bulging muscles appear all the more comical. Billy imagines Derico would need to stand on his tip-toes to order a slice of pizza because he could not see over the countertop.

Billy is fairly certain Frank Derico's deposit is his next target, but he still needs to do some surveillance of the bank branch on 23rd Street and of Derico to be certain it would be an easy hold up. Billy shuts down his desktop for the night, puts on his blazer and heads out to the Christmas party, despite it being the middle of summer. Even though the bank that Billy works for the world's largest financial institution, it is too cheap to pay for a large party venue in Manhattan during the prime month of December for its annual Christmas party. Christmas drinks on the bank's dime always have to wait until July, though Christmas bonuses are doled out each March. This year the bank has rented out the Museum of Natural History to host the party, it's a nice event space, but the bank is so cheap that no significant others are invited or allowed. This is strictly an employee only event.

Billy knows that showing his face at the corporate Christmas party is risky since some of these people are the very same people who he has either robbed, or might one day rob, but Billy isn't too worried about being recognized since he uses facial prosthetics during his hold ups. Billy stands beside the bones of a dinosaur and sips a beer with his brother-in-law Sven, his sister Eva, and another coworker Ed. All of them work with Billy in some capacity at the bank and none of them know that Billy had ever been on the wagon, let alone that he has recently fallen off the wagon. Sven is the C.E.O. of the North American bank and Eva is a power broker with high net worth clients at the private bank. Both have ritzy offices on Park Avenue at 50th Street that are furnished with ancient Incan and Mayan works of art that were looted decades ago. Ed is one of the bank's top IT guys, who grew up with Sven and has known him since they were little kids. The four of them quietly drink and walk around the museum together, taking in the exhibits and the hired magicians who are performing sleight of hand tricks, as other performers are dressed up in furry costumes and are pretending to be animals. They run into Don, the big boss, who is a drunken 50-something year old billionaire with political aspirations, whose job title is C.E.O. of the publicly traded worldwide bank. Don walks up to them, "Eva! Didn't I always tell you that Sven was no good for you?"

  Billy and Ed are introduced to Don and it is like the three of them are old friends. After chatting for a bit, Don goes on his merry way to keep mingling. Billy and Ed both decide to ditch Eva and Sven because their married status is inhibiting their God given right to get their drink on. As they say "see you later" to Sven and Eva, Sven warns Billy to not go beer-for-beer with Ed, because doing so always ends up badly for everyone who attempts to go toe-to-toe with Ed's alcohol tolerance. Ed is well over six foot and does not feel alcohol easily.

   Billy immediately ignores Sven's warning and goes beer-for-beer with Ed. After all, the beers are all free. They traipse through a sea of corporate casual that is colliding with corporate professional suit and tie. They quickly down several beers and are looking for people that they each work with when suddenly a tree that is planted in a corner gets up and walks directly in front of them to the other side of a doorway. A woman shrieks as Billy and Ed cannot believe their eyes. The tree is actually a man on stilts dressed up as a tree. They are both amazed at seeing the tree-man scare people, so they stand nearby drinking as the tree-man stands against a wall, silent and still, waiting to trick more unsuspecting people. After a good five minutes, tree-man starts moving again, which makes more people scream, and makes Billy and Ed laugh to the point where Billy spills beer on his shoes and lower pant leg. Going beer for beer with Ed has made Billy quickly become a sloppy drunk.

   Cell phone service is currently blocked at the museum tonight, due to Don's paranoia about a disgruntled employee planting an IED near him, and using a cell phone to activate it and kill him with it. Because of Don's paranoia, Billy and Ed continue to get drinks and move room to room in the vast museum as they try to locate coworkers in their stone-age surroundings and black boxes that block cell tower signals. They keep looking everywhere and Billy is now three sheets to the wind.

Billy finally spots a coworker and screams "KENNY" while giving Kenny a big hug, as if Kenny was lost at sea for months.   Billy turns around to tell Ed that he has found Kenny, but forgets all about it in the process of turning, so when he turns back and sees Kenny once again screams "KENNY."   Billy does this a solid ten times before Kenny's constant affirmations that Billy has already spotted him sink in. Sven's brother, Pete, who works with Ed, shows up and tells Billy that he will drive him home at the end of the night. With an open bar and a pocket full of taxi money that doesn't need to be spent, Billy continues to drink with Ed before finally realizing that his bladder needs to be emptied. Billy tells the guys that he is hitting the restroom and that he will meet them back in that specific dance party room that has a brontosaurus instead of a disco ball.

Billy soon begins to drift in and out of a blackout on his way to find the nearest restroom. He doesn't consciously realize it. He never does. His brain somehow tells him to stop off for more beer because the nearest restroom is too hard to find. Who is Billy to turn down free drinks when he is already too drunk to stand without bumping into other people? As Billy continues his restroom quest, he goes through several rooms lined with bones, up a flight of stairs and past a set of eight people dressed as wooden soldiers who are marching through the museum before finally finding the restroom.

After finishing up in the restroom, Billy takes a moment to remember how to get back to the brontosaurus dance floor. He remembers a flight of stairs, multiple rooms, marching wooden soldiers and bumping into people while ordering more beer. He is certain that these are all things that need to happen once again in order to get back to the dinosaur dance party, but he is not sure the order in which it needs to happen or even the direction from which he came. Billy stands and looks around for a moment and takes the party in. Some people are wearing ties, while others aren't, but they all look as though they lead boring lives and are on the brink of death, Billy thinks to himself. After gazing at the crowd all around him, Billy begins to walk the way that he suspects is the correct way and soon comes upon the wooden soldiers. Billy can't help but laugh like a drunken fool at the men pretending to be wooden soldiers all marching in unison, which distracts him from the task at hand of trying to find his coworkers and his free ride home. When the wooden soldiers stop their bit, Billy is really lost, but figures that he will mull his intra-museum directions over while sipping on another beer. He repeats this process in several rooms and then doesn't know what is happening anymore. Billy continues along his merry way completely blacked out.

Eventually Billy hears a man say his name several times. Then Billy feels hands on his face as his name is screamed into his ear. Billy's eyes were open the entire time, but his vision finally reactivates and connects with the proper spot inside of his drunken brain. He finds himself standing in the middle of a crowded room, with a man named Rivers standing before him holding his head straight. Rivers works on the floor below Billy and the guys who work for Rivers call Billy "Little Rivers" because they look very much alike, though Rivers was a foot taller and ten years older than Billy. Rivers looks at Billy like he is a little brother.

"You okay, man?"

"Yeah…"

Billy looks to the right of Rivers and sees Don the billionaire double fisting bottles of champagne and laughing.

"What are you doing?"

"Oh… I was just going to thank Don for throwing such a wonderful party."

"I don't think that you should do that. Bill, you better not go near Don like this."

"Okay. I won't then."

"How are you getting home?"

"Pete Grahlman is driving me."

"Do you know where he is?"

"No, but I'm looking for him."

"Well, if you can't find him, you can crash on my sofa. Just get in a cab and go to 560 East 68th Street."

"Thanks man. A cab to 650 68th."

"No, 560 East 68th."

"568 East 68th. Got it."

"Bill, are you with me? It's 560 East 68th Street. Say it with me."

"560 East 68th Street."

"Remember that address, I think that you're going to need it."

Billy walks away repeating Rivers' address, but then he sees another table of free beer and becomes distracted. Billy is saying all sorts of different number combinations aloud and is lost as could be. He then blacks out again and is once again continuing to walk around with a beer in hand during his blackout.

Billy is wandering lost in the blackout for 20 minutes. Eventually a clown walks up to him and puts his arm around Billy, under his shoulders as Billy puts his right arm over the clown's shoulder. He is a literal clown, white face, red nose, big shoes, funky clothing and crazy red hair, but Billy doesn't know that it is a clown, because his eyes aren't seeing, but his ears are still somewhat working.

"Hey buddy, are you lost?"

"Yeah."

"Where are you going? Maybe I can help."

"I'm trying to find Pete Grahlman."

"Let's go find him."

The clown begins to walk Billy in a big circle around a bench in the middle of a large room, before repeating his questions as a gag to those who are watching them, assuming that Billy is too drunk to remember, but Billy does remember... after the fourth time.

"Hey buddy, are you lost?"

Billy's eyes reconnect. He realizes that it is a clown and that the clown is walking him in a giant circle while people are laughing at them.

"Are you lost buddy? Maybe I can help."

"Pete Grahlman! Bring me to Pete Grahlman." Billy says, before blacking out again.

Not knowing when to quit, the clown asks yet again if Billy is lost. This causes Billy to unknowingly tighten his right arm around the clown to the point where he has the clown in a headlock.

Billy is indignant and just keeps repeatedly shouting "PETE GRAHLMAN!"

"I don't know any Pete Grahlman. I'm sorry. Please let me go."

"PETE GRAHLMAN! PETE GRAHLMAN! PETE GRAHLMAN!"

"Stop! Stop! Stop! I don't know him!"

"PETE GRAHLMAN! PETE..."

Suddenly Billy's legs are no longer on the ground and he is floating through the air, sans clown in a headlock. Billy looks to his right and sees Kenny and then to his left and sees Pete Grahlman.

"Hey Pete, I was just looking for you."

"I know, Bill. Half of the people here know that you were looking for me."

Pete and Kenny carry Billy to the whale room and Billy finds everyone who he was looking for, but Billy can't stay. Pete realizes that Billy is far too drunk and acting like a fool. Pete tells Billy that they need to leave, and for the life of him, Billy can't figure out why. There are still two hours of open bar left to drink up.

Pete has Billy hold onto his shoulders so that he can navigate them through the crowd. Each time one of Pete's coworkers says hello to him, Billy makes sure to say an even bigger hello back to them, which causes Pete to tell Billy to stop saying hello to people.

The next morning, Billy heads into work feeling refreshed and rested. This is part of the fortune of being Billy and getting wasted. Hangovers don't occur. After Billy key cards himself onto the floor of his office, he sees all of his coworkers looking at him with big grins. Billy opens the door, wishes everyone a good morning and receives a raucous laugh from everyone. It had been that kind of a night.

Chapter 4

A steady rain is falling upon the city as Billy sits and waits for Frank Derico at a coffee shop across the street from Derico's apartment. Billy sits and thinks about how a steady rain tends to make New York City cleanish. Rain almost cleans the city, but the city will never actually be clean. Even after a hard rain, the city is only as clean as a toothless, drug addicted prostitute who took a cold shower after a busy night of hooking and shooting up heroin. Billy eats a croissant and drinks an iced coffee at a table near the window facing Derico's apartment. Nobody around Billy can possibly guess that he isn't simply having a snack and that he is instead stalking $40,000 in what he hopes is easy cash. A baby cries off in a corner of the coffee shop that has too many strollers for Billy's taste. Billy wonders if he will ever want to, or even be able to, have children of his own. He knows that he will have to get his semi-functional alcoholic personality cleaned up once again before anything remotely like kids can come into the picture.

   Yellow cabs zip past the window, ferrying people who don't have to be in an office at one o'clock on a Monday afternoon. Billy wonders if any of these yellow cabs have any bank robbers in them. As 1:30 approaches, Billy begins to wonder if Derico spends his Sunday nights and Monday mornings at a place other than his own apartment.

   Billy crumples up the wax paper that his croissant came wrapped in and is ready to give up the day's surveillance when Derico exits the door to his apartment and steps out onto Park Avenue. Derico is holding a paper bag that Billy assumes has roughly $40,000 in it. In person, Frank Derico's height is even more comedic than in the photos. Derico's overcompensating body language reeks of confidence on the surface, but Derico is a tall man in a short man's body that isn't going to grow any taller. Derico walks with his arms overly extended outward from his hips to make himself appear bigger than he actually is, and keeps his head cranked all the way back on his neck, so that should he ever come across a fellow his own height he can give off the illusion of looking down at him. Derico's actual walk is somewhat cartoonish. His walk gives off the aura of Derico having a frozen salmon in the back of his pants along with wet toenails and that white foam from nail salons still being stuck between his toes.

Though Derico is by far the shortest person on the street, Billy is easily able to follow him visually, since Derico has the shiniest and loudest outfit on of anyone within a five block radius. As Derico enters the bank around the corner and across the street from his apartment, Billy exits the coffee shop. Billy opens his umbrella and casually crosses over to the bank. He stops at the window and pretends to adjust his necktie in the reflection. As he looks inside, he watches as Derico is the second of three people on Mandi Whalen's line for commercial transactions. His first impression of Mandi Whalen is that she will be an easy mark and that the layout of the branch truly is ideal for a quick in and out job.

Billy throws his iced coffee into the garbage can and heads over towards the subway. There's no way for him to catch a cab in the rain. He heads back to his office.

As Billy walks through the corridor to his cube, his boss, Chris, catches him.

"Bill. Come into my office."

"Howdy Chris. What's up?"

"Another celebrity has begun hocking a new weight loss pill on late night commercials. I need you to pull all of the transactions of both the pill company and the celebrity. I want you to also dig a little into everyone that they either received payment from or made a payment to. This pill looks like another drug money front. I'll email you the client name."

"Sounds good, give me a few days and I'll have everything you need Chris."

Billy heads to his desk, dreading his new task of pulling the transactions and looking into yet another diet pill company. Diet pill companies that pop up overnight with infomercials and have celebrity endorsements are almost always a front for laundering large amounts of cash.

Billy logs into his computer, flicks the snake plant on his desk with hopes of it popping out more oxygen and reads the email:

Bill, Jessica Lopez: account # 555-95681. Product name "E-Z LOSE WEIGHT KEEP IT OFF" Need it done by Thursday.

Billy begins the grunt work. Sure enough, pop star Jessica Lopez has received a hefty payment to be the face of this new weight loss product that likely does nothing. Further transactions reveal that Lopez has also been receiving structured payments just below $10,000 from several individuals who don't appear to be on the up and up. One such individual is named Frank Derico, the very same Frank Derico. Derico is also showing up as a signer on the account for the diet pill. Billy takes a look at the account for Derico's club. A deposit for $38,800 was logged earlier in the afternoon at 1:33PM. Mandi Whalen has proven herself to be a speedy teller when it comes to counting large amounts of cash, especially fast when considering that she only makes $32,000 a year for her efficient work. Billy knows that this next haul will be a good one.

Chapter 5

The phone rings. Billy picks up the receiver and hears Mia's lovely voice on the other end. It's 7:30 in the evening. Billy is still working on the Jessica Lopez account. Mia is trying to invite herself over to Billy's apartment for when she gets off of her bartending shift at 4AM. As much as Billy wants to see Mia, he already has plans tonight that don't involve Mia and he doesn't want her to find out about them.

"I'm staying late at work tonight and need to be up ridiculously early to come back in for a big case that my boss wants done. So I need to take a rain check. I want to see you soon, maybe tomorrow?"

Plans between Mia and Billy are made for the next night and Billy logs off of his desktop for the night. Billy goes off to meet Janet, who is a childhood friend of his and visiting the city from California. Both Billy and Janet have had crushes on one another several times over the years, but one of them has always been in a monogamous relationship whenever Janet has rolled through town in the past. They have always stayed in contact but couldn't ever meet out of fear of breaking the trust of a relationship. Today though, neither of them is involved in a monogamous relationship. They are both anxious and giddy with excitement about what the night might bring to them.

The rain has ended and Billy hails a cab to the rendezvous with

Janet. Billy watches the city pass while he heads downtown. He silently thinks about his eight years of sobriety, his falling off the wagon, blackouts and the early morning hospital visit that he has endured since hitting the bottle again. Billy tends to binge. He catches glimpses of strangers from the speedy taxi and wonders in the city that never sleeps how many others are struggling with alcohol the way he is. He can't quit now, though he desperately wants to. The time just isn't right to quit. He's having too much fun reliving his out of control past that he once thought was buried and gone.

Billy gets out of the cab at West 3rd and MacDougal Street. Janet is sitting inside of the pizza shop, smiles and waves hello. Billy's face flushes red. He hasn't seen Janet since she left the city the summer after her college graduation. She looks even more beautiful now than she did all those years ago. Billy immediately falls in love with Janet once again at first sight. Bright eyed and bushy tailed, they quickly walk to one another and embrace in a long hug. Billy breathes Janet's scent in and is head over heels for her. Billy knows that he should end up with Janet, but that he isn't prepared for the possibility of settling down with "the one" just yet.

They walk down MacDougal and head into a basement cafe that has cover bands playing music for tourists. They enter the cafe a little after eight and don't leave until after two in the morning. During this time, they drink away any inhibitions that they've had regarding one another and have held onto since childhood. They walk out onto Minetta Street, which is a crooked street that hides a buried creek. The sky is now clear of all clouds and the smooth night air feels cool to their warm skin. They drunkenly try to say goodnight. One kiss leads to another and a hot and heavy make-out session takes place at the curve of the street. The years of flirtation and sexual innuendo between them are finally hitting a head and it is decided that they finally need to have one another on a bed somewhere.

"Do you want to come to my place?" Janet asks.

"Without a doubt." Billy replies, even though Janet's place is actually her mother's house, which means that Janet's disapproving and intimidating mother who sleeps with a loaded gun on her nightstand will be asleep across the hall from Janet's bedroom while they get naked. Janet's mother has always terrified Billy. If she catches them in a compromising position, Billy's life will be in jeopardy and he will have to jump out of the bedroom's second floor window and run until he's in Florida. Billy and Janet drunkenly meander further downtown while stopping several times to make out. They walk until they find Janet's mother's car at the beginning of 6th Avenue, they get in it and find themselves in a giggle fit of anticipation. Billy still doesn't have the foresight to think about detouring Janet back to his apartment to avoid the possibility of getting shot by Janet's mother.

Janet drives under a lot of influence through Manhattan and Brooklyn. She never drives drunk and never drinks so much, but being around Billy has her doing things that she wouldn't normally do. While stopped at a red light in Brooklyn, along Hamilton Avenue, they reach across the center console for one another and kiss and embrace. Billy's hand slips between Janet's legs. He feels through Janet's jeans that she is hot and wet between her legs. Janet spreads her legs and moans as Billy caresses her sweet spot over her jeans while they kiss with a lot of tongue. They stay at that traffic light for three red lights before finally continuing back to Janet's.

Janet pulls into the open space at the curb cut to her mother's driveway and parks the car. She then realizes that she has forgotten the keys to her mother's house inside of her childhood bedroom.

"I'm going to get my sister to sneak us in. She's visiting Brooklyn too. Don't say anything so that you don't wake up my mom."

Janet clinks the car key on the front window until her sister Amy wakes up on the couch in a daze and lets them in with a smile. Amy quietly mouths, "you two."

Janet leads Billy quietly up the stairs and into her childhood bedroom and locks the door. Billy's heart is beating to the max at the realization of finally being with Janet. Billy is terrified about sleeping with Janet. The thought of possibly ruining their friendship scares Billy, but he is also worried sick that her mother will hear them, kick down the door, catch them mid-coitus and then shoot him until she is out of ammo.

Janet's bedroom is barely illuminated by the little streetlight that is bleeding in through the tie-dyed curtains that she decided to hang during her hippie phase in high school. Despite such little light, Billy can see that Janet looks absolutely beautiful. Her kisses feel like heaven, her curvy chest, tummy and butt all feel marvelous. Billy knows that this is the moment that he has waited 15 years for and is making sure to enjoy each and every second and sensation of it. Billy and Janet quickly realize that they are in major trouble when they notice that they are dumb enough to both finally be available, naked in bed and without a condom. Billy knows that he is clean and Janet knows that she is clean. So they give into one another's temptation and place far more trust with one another than they should in this situation.

"Just remember to pull out." Janet whispers into Billy's ear as she pulls him inside of her.

Janet rides on top of Billy while he thrusts with eager participation. They are both wearing nothing but smiles ear to ear. Several moments later, Janet whispers again into Billy's ear, "Oh my God. Shhh. Stop moving."

They stay quiet and still for a minute before Billy asks, "what's going on?"

"I think that I heard my mother knocking on the door."

Billy feels lucky that he didn't instantly poop Janet's bed from the fear that goes through his mind at the thought of Janet's disapproving gun-toting mother being at the door. He then thinks back to all of the sounds that has been hearing and doesn't remember any knocking. All that he heard was the internal sound of his own heart beating the loudest that it has ever beat. It is beating so loud that it sounds as though it is trying to burst out of his chest. THUMP! THUMP! THUMP!

Billy assumes the loud beats are caused by the trifecta of excitement due to finally being with Janet, the bareback ride that Janet is literally giving him and knowing that her mom can burst through the door and kill him at any given moment. They lay still as Billy listens to his heart beat.

"Is that what you hear?"

"Yeah."

"That's my heart beating."

"Holy fuck."

They continue at it until they are both satiated with the other. They then take turns finishing each other off while screaming into a pillow to muffle the sound. Billy just found in Janet a high that equals holding up banks and is saddened to know that it is bittersweet because it cannot last, since Janet is returning to California the next afternoon.

Chapter 6

Billy and Mia are at her friend Christian's mother's Tribeca loft for a party. Christian's mother is an artist who has had the apartment since 1972 and pays a mere $437 a month in rent. The apartment would go for no less than ten times that if it were to hit market rate. The loft is a fifth floor walk up that spans the length of a building that was built to be a factory in 1890. It has dark wooden floorboards, floor to ceiling bookshelves, ratty throw carpets line the hallway and it is dimly lit as incense burns into the air. Paintings, all the work of Christian's mother, line the wall space wherever there aren't shelves. Billy's first thought of the place is that Christian's mother is one lucky failed artist.

Billy and Mia are drinking glasses of whiskey the size of fists as they dance to the selections played from the loft's large vinyl collection. The Bee Gees are blasting out of the stereo when Christian takes out his old BB gun and thinks that the present moment is the best time to play with it. Christian isn't sure if the BB gun still works so he test fires it out the back window. He finds out that it does work. Christian then tries to hit targets within the loft. BB pellets are whizzing past Billy's eyes and then bouncing off bookshelves. Billy's eyes bug out of his head at the thought of Christian literally shooting Billy's eyes out, so he stands quietly with his hands over his eyes, waiting for Christian to finish firing off the rest of his ammo. A pellet lands directly on Billy's left hand and stings him. A red welt instantly appears. Billy laughs and doesn't feel the true pain that he should be feeling due to the whiskey.

"Put this empty beer can on top of your head and see if I can shoot it off." Christian tells Billy, as if this is the best thing in the world to be doing. Billy stands still with the beer can on top of his head, and waits to be shot again like a drunken fool. Christian steadies, takes aim and is about to squeeze the trigger when his mother takes the gun away from him.

"Oh, come on mom. It's not like I would even come close to shooting Billy. The gun has always had a sharp left hook to its shots. You know this!"

Billy's mother offers the guests pot brownies that she spent the afternoon baking. Ever the hippie, she knows that pot brownies will keep Christian calm and the party festive.

Billy hasn't done pot since well before he went into treatment for substance abuse. It has been more than eight years since he's done pot, despite Mia's near constant requests for him to smoke up with her. The two fist-sized glasses of whiskey that Billy has had this night allows him to give into Mia's peer pressure. Billy eats two large brownies that each had a quarter ounce of weed in them. The only other time that Billy ate a pot brownie, he found himself unable to move for hours and time felt as though it had stopped and gone in reverse. Billy is thankful to discover that these brownies don't have the same effect on him as the first one did so many years ago. It is the perfect high to go with his drunken buzz. Billy feels good and mellow. It is the best that he has felt in years.

Mia sits Billy down and begs him to allow her to tell him who some of the other people that she has been having sex with because Billy knows them. The topic immediately kills Billy's high. He begs Mia to not tell him who they are because he really doesn't want to know who she has been with. He doesn't want to know because he knows that he has actual feelings for Mia. Though Mia isn't his only girl, Billy thinks the world of her, and understands that he is falling for her, despite knowing deep down that the two of them will never work out.

Despite his pleas, Mia tells Billy the names of three of the men whom she is having sex with on the side and also informs Billy of a threesome that she recently had with folks from the bar where she works at as a bartender. Billy immediately feels sick from the news.

For Billy, hearing this news is equivalent to having a grenade explode inside of his head. Even though Billy has ladies on the side, the one cardinal rule in his relationship with Mia has always been to not throw the interlopers into the face of the other. Billy is deeply hurt. He moves off to a couch in a dark corner of the loft. He is sad and begins to feel sleepy from the effects of the whiskey mixing with the pot. He wants to have the world around him disappear and wake up so that he will know that this night is nothing but a bad dream.

Mia sees how hurt Billy is and moves over to him. Mia takes Billy's face and begins to make out feverishly with him on the couch in the corner. They are making out and groping one another to the point that anyone who passes them feels uncomfortable at the sight of their display of affection.

Mia tells Billy that she suddenly needs to go to the bathroom.

"Should I join you?" Billy asks, with a devilish grin.

"Yes, you should." Mia grabs Billy's hand and leads him to a tiny bathroom off of the hallway that is opposite from the kitchen that is full of people drinking, laughing and smoking. Billy locks the door behind them and they pick up from where we left off on the couch. The bathroom is tiny. There is barely enough room for both Billy and Mia to stand. There is a mirror hanging above the sink that displays everything in it backwards. The floor tiles are old and are no longer cemented to the floor. They are merely resting on the ground and with each step that Billy and Mia take, the tiles clink against the floor.

Their bottoms are soon naked as their hips gyrate into one another. Billy tries to put a condom on, but in his stupor, it doesn't make it on. It falls to the floor beneath them. Billy begins to blackout as he props Mia up against the brick wall while they are one. Billy's last conscious thought before his eyes go black is the realization that the brick wall might cut Mia's astounding bubble-butt, so he decides that he needs to protect it from any scrapes or bruise, in the heat of the moment Billy grabs two hands full of Mia's butt, using his hands as a cover to both protect Mia's tush and to help with their coitus maneuvering. As Billy grabs hold of Mia's butt, he thinks that his hand covering the butt technique is genius and is on par with Einstein.

Mia moans while sucking on Billy's neck to keep her carnal

sounds to a minimum. Then a fist bangs on the door that scares the life out of them. Billy comes to.

"Uh... I'm in here... It's going to be a while. I'm shitting."

"Uh... yeah. I'm shitting too." Mia blurts out, as they laugh and continue to hump, unknowingly ripping the skin off of the back of Billy's hands, as they scrape back and forth and up and down against the brick wall. By the time they exit the bathroom and try to mingle in the party again, Billy feels as though everyone there knows what they had been doing in the bathroom. Worse yet, Billy's hands look as though they lost a fight with a squirrel, but he doesn't yet notice them.

Chapter 7

It is Wednesday morning when Billy and Mia leave from Christian's mother's loft. Billy wishes that he had much more sleep, but goes straight to work in the clothes that he wore the day before. Mia is going to her apartment in a three story building that is leaning heavily over onto the empty lot next door in Bushwick. The sight of the bright sun makes Billy think about how evil the sun can be with its bright warmth at times. While they say goodbye, Mia notices Billy's scraped hands.

"Oh my God. What happened to your hands? It looks like you got into a fight with a chipmunk."

Billy looks at the back of his hands. He sees red welts and small bloody scrapes on them. He is clueless as to how they got there.

"I remember a BB gun, two pot cookies and having sex with you in the bathroom. Did Christian have a chipmunk in there too?"

"No."

Neither one of them can remember how the scrapes and red marks got there. When Billy gets to work he concludes that his life has been quickly spinning out of control since he fell off the wagon. He realizes that he needs to take it easy on this day and that he really does need to sleep in a bed tonight. As he sits in front of the computer screen, he feels that it is extra bright today, so bright that it makes him feel as though he is looking directly into the sun. Lights are Billy's nemesis of the day, but he needs to finish the

Jessica Lopez account for his boss, Chris, and also needs to run an errand in the form of stalking Frank Derico for a second time. The stalking of Derico is not so much a thing so that Billy will have better intelligence on the guy, but to ensure that Billy will have a smooth bank robbery, because Billy is fascinated by Derico and cannot stop laughing when he thinks about how short and comical Derico's stature is. Plus, Billy needs a good laugh to get him through the exhaustion that he is currently feeling. Each key stroke, mouse click and transaction that Billy makes, causes him to feel as though the weight of the world is on his shoulders. He just wants to curl up and go to sleep. Billy trudges through the morning and by noon he has finished the Jessica Lopez account. He files the report and sends it to Chris.

All that Billy wants is a bed to lie in, but he is only halfway through the day. He can take the subway down to Derico's, but is worried about falling asleep on it. If he falls asleep on the subway, he won't wake up until he's out near the end of the line in Crown Heights. Billy decides to put off Derico for another day. He knows that he needs something to help him through this exhaustion, so he goes over to the far side of the floor of his office building and spots the bank's North American Chief Operating Officer's assistant, Donna, sitting at her desk. Billy knows that Donna has a secret sleeping spot because she told him about it after he slept with her after last year's Christmas party.

The secret sleep spot is the barely used corner office of an executive whose regular office is down on Wall Street. Donna is the only one with the key to the office and has boxes set up to completely block the view of everything beneath the desk from the hallway. She has used this particular office to sleep away her hangovers since she was hired more than 11 years ago. Billy quietly begs Donna to give him the key so that he can go down for a nap. Donna doesn't want to let anyone else sleep there for fear of losing her perfectly hidden in plain sight jerry-rigged bed. Donna isn't budging on allowing Billy to sleep there. Donna's boss, the C.O.O., hears the commotion outside of his office and asks for both Billy and Donna to step into his office.

"Donna, close the door."

His corner office is large and gaudy with several marble busts. Billy thinks that he has just opened a whole can of worms that he didn't want and that he is in for a screaming.

"Donna, give Bill the key to the office that you've been sleeping in three times a week since you started here."

Donna looks at her boss in a complete state of shock. How could he have known?

"Donna, don't look at me like I wouldn't notice what happens directly outside of my office. Bill, return the key to Donna when your nap has concluded. And Bill, I'm going to tell Sven that this nap of yours wipes my owing him a bottle of scotch off the table from our last round of golf. You might owe him one now."

Billy gets the key and opens the office. Behind the wall of boxes is a soft roll of foam strewn across the floor that can be used as a mattress, a blanket and a small roll of bubble wrap that fits perfectly under his head as a pillow. He gets beneath the desk and lays across the foam on his right side. The bubble wrap is surprisingly comfy. Billy notices that this office is built better than most of the others on the floor. It is much quieter than the other offices. Billy can't hear anything from the main cubicle area and suspects that the executive had a sound barrier installed. Donna's not so hidden nap location is a rather ingenious one.

As Billy settles in to drift off to sleep, he looks at the scratches on the back of his hands and is still having trouble remembering what had happened to them. The previous night is a giant ball of fuzzy memory. He thinks good thoughts about how he and Mia fooled around in the bathroom and begins to drift off. Suddenly it comes to him. He realizes how the scratches got onto his hands. He quickly sits up, not remembering that he is beneath a desk in an office and bangs his head against the bottom of the desk. Billy has knocked himself out cold and doesn't know it. The only known key to this mostly unused office is in his pocket. Billy will stay under the desk until his body decides to awaken.

Chapter 8

Billy wakes a little after 7PM. He looks at his watch and gasps at how much time has passed. He only intended for a 30 minute nap, not seven hours. His head feels rattled from hitting it on the desk. He looks at his cell phone and sees 15 missed calls from Donna. He rolls out from beneath the desk. He feels good and well rested, aside from what he assumes is a newly concussed head.

Billy takes the key down to Donna's desk and is surprised to see that she is still sitting at her desk. Donna sees Billy and gives him an annoyed look. Donna pulls Billy down so that she can speak quietly into his ear.

"Bill, what the fuck were you thinking by taking the entire afternoon off and sleeping in my spot? I was tired and couldn't use it because you weren't picking up your phone."

"Donna, I'm sorry. I hit my head on the bottom of the desk and knocked myself out. I think that I have a concussion."

"Bullshit."

"Here. Give me your hand. Feel this." Billy rubs Donna's fingertip across the bump beneath his hairline.

"Ouch. That feels like it hurts. You okay?"

"I'll be fine. Thank you the concern."

"Bill, a bunch of us will be going out to the Pot for drinks because Laura is moving back to Utah. You're welcome to join if you'd like."

"I'll meet you there."

Billy walks into the men's room. He looks into the mirror and sees a stranger looking back at him. Billy's reflection looks familiar, but the man behind the eyes looks different and unrecognizable to himself. Billy knows that he is in the middle of a downward spiral and is fairly out of control. He splashes water across his face. It feels invigorating. Billy doesn't know how to fix himself, so he assumes that he should just go on the ride and see where it continues to take him.

As Billy is drying his face off Chris walks into the bathroom. Chris greets Bill with a big smile.

"Bill, excellent work on the Jessica Lopez accounts."

"Thank you, Chris."

Chris is now standing at a urinal, fly unzipped, doing his business and keeps the conversation going. Billy is always disgusted when his coworkers do this.

"Don't stay working too late tonight, Bill. Make sure to come join us for a drink or two at the Pot for Laura's farewell."

"I just need to wrap up this last account for the night and I'll meet you at the Pot."

"Great news. It'll be good to see my workaholic relax a bit." Chris says, as he jump shakes his penis at the urinal before putting it back into his underwear and then zips up. Chris doesn't wash his hands. "See you in a bit."

Billy returns to his desk. There aren't any important voicemails or emails waiting for him. Not even a handwritten note from anyone looking for him. It appears as though Billy got away with the perfect nap. Billy logs off of his desktop for the night and heads over to the Pot.

Billy walks into the Pot alone and sees approximately 20 people that work on his floor standing around with drinks in their hands. The Pot is an Irish pub that has crossed over to a dive bar. The Pot is a couple of blocks from Billy's office at the farthest east side of Midtown and hasn't had many updates since the Irish mob imploded decades earlier. The Irish mob had used the Pot as a gathering place once all of their spots in Hell's Kitchen became too hot for them. The wood of the bar is old and dark and has not been taken care of. Old men line the bar. They look like they haven't moved from their stools in decades and have grown roots. They are watching Wheel of Fortune with the sound off via a projector.

There are also several groups of nine to five people who are trying to settle their bar tabs so that they can commute back to Long Island, New Jersey, and Westchester. Billy knows that he cannot allow himself to drink to excess and make a fool of himself once again. He already did that once around coworkers recently and doesn't want the stigma to last. Billy knows that he needs to keep his professional image together despite the fact that he knows that he is quickly unraveling at each and every seam.

Billy is greeted warmly by the crowd. Some of whom have been drinking since 5PM and are three sheets to the wind. Billy is good and doesn't let himself overindulge in alcohol as the crowd dwindles down, leaving only the hardcore drinkers still at the bar. Only six people remain of the Laura crowd. Laura left about an hour ago, Donna went home with the new guy from Billy's department and Chris had only one drink before leaving for his house in Westchester. Three young guys remain: Dean, Brian and Billy. They are all their own doppelgangers. People often confuse them while passing in the hallway since they are all of the same age, height and build, at about 5'10" and 190lbs with fair skin and light brown hair. The three remaining women are: Jackie, Sheila and Janelle. The three ladies all look nothing alike. Jackie is Chris' administrative assistant. She is a foxy 40-something redhead who has always given Billy sultry looks with her blue eyes. Sheila and Janelle are both about 30 years old. Janelle is another V.P.'s admin and is by far the hottest woman on Billy's floor. She is a Peruvian beauty, married and gathering her belongings to leave the bar. Sheila is one of Billy's fellow analysts and is as white as the whitest of bread. She is in the middle of the road in the looks department, a solid six on her best day and is engaged to be married.

All three ladies go outside for one last smoke together before Janelle leaves. Billy, Dean and Brian comment amongst themselves about how hot Janelle looks. She is the perfect ten of their workplace and an impossible woman to score. The ladies come back in and Janelle says good bye to the group. Nobody is going to get to touch the untouchable tonight. After Janelle leaves, Jackie and Sheila immediately go back outside for another smoke. All three men find this back to back cigarette as a bit odd. Several minutes later, Jackie and Sheila return with devilish grins on their faces from ear to ear. They clearly have something that they want to tell the guys and race towards them. Billy wonders if maybe the ladies saw someone run into the side of a taxi or something of that ilk.

"Sheila and I were talking outside and have an idea. What do you say we all go home together and the three of you fuck the two of us?" Jackie says bluntly with a big smile and beaming eyes.

The three men stand there quietly. They are nervously silent and try to not make any eye contact with anyone else, but they each sneak looks at the other's faces to see how this is going to proceed.

"The three of you take on the two of us. What do you say?" Sheila says calmly, as if she is merely ordering a bagel with lox and cream cheese on a boring Monday morning. As if she doesn't have an engagement ring on. As if this is a normal every day type of proposition to be asking anyone, let alone coworkers.

"Umm… uhh… uhh…" Are the only collective thoughts that Billy, Dean and Brian are able to verbalize. They are left speechless. Billy isn't sure if Jackie and Sheila are serious about a random orgy with coworkers and he realizes that such a sexual escapade is a bit much for him. The boys' lack of ability to say anything kills the orgy invite.

"Okay, well who wants to come home and fuck me?" Jackie asks, with what is now only a hopeful smile on her face. The three guys are still left speechless. Nobody says a word, but Billy has wanted to sleep with Jackie for years, so he raises his hand as a silent volunteer. Jackie immediately grabs hold of Billy's hand and begins pulling him to the door. "We're leaving now."

Billy is pulled through the bar and out the door so fast that he now knows that they had been serious about having an interoffice orgy.

"I wasn't sure if you two were serious in there."

"I know that we don't live too far from one another in Brooklyn. Is my place alright?"

"Fine with me. Where do you even live?"

"Dyker Heights. Are you sure that you want to go through with this?"

"Hell yeah! I thought you were hot ever since I first met you. I'd love to fuck you." It is the one and only time that Billy knowingly says something out loud as if he is in a porno. Upon hearing his words, even he is shocked by them.

"Good. Because I want a good fuck from you."

Billy takes a moment to replay that last remark that Jackie just said and begins to immediately think that he very well may have gotten himself into a situation that is a little bit over his head, but Billy still goes along with Jackie because he doesn't know if there will ever be another opportunity to jump into bed with her. Jackie continues, "By the way, none of this ever happened. Don't mention it to anyone at work. If you do, I will deny it and make your life a living hell."

Billy and Jackie hop on the F train. Shortly thereafter, Billy realizes that he has forgotten his man-purse at the bar. In the drunken rush of being dragged out of the bar Billy forgot that he had brought it with him.

"Fuck, I forgot my bag at the bar."

"We can't go back there. Call up Dean or Brian and see if they can bring it to work tomorrow."

Billy and Jackie briefly exit the subway at Rock Center to make the phone call. Neither Dean nor Brian hear their cell phones in the loud bar, so Billy calls information to get through to the bar, "Hi, I was drinking at the end of the bar by the TV and just left. Any chance my friends Dean or Brian are still there?"

"Gimme a sec young fella." The old man working the bar tells him with an Irish brogue.

"Hello?" A shocked Dean asks.

"Dude! I left my bag at the bar. Do you see it and can you bring it to work tomorrow?"

"It's a man-purse, right?"

"Yes."

"Are you really going to go have sex with Jackie?"

"Yes, I'm pretty sure."

"Awesome. And I found your bag. I'll bring it in tomorrow. Have fun."

Billy and Jackie go back down into the subway. This time they hop on the D train and head out to Brooklyn.

"What's your girlfriend going to think of you doing me?"

"I don't have a girlfriend."

"Really? I've seen you meeting up with the same girl several times after work. She's pretty and you two always look as though you are an item."

"Looks can deceive."

Upon arrival at Jackie's apartment, she gives Billy a quick tour of her two bedroom place, which he cannot help but notice is spotless. They crack open beers, watch some Fallon and are unsure of how to proceed. When their beers are about done, Jackie finally breaks the ice, "Are we going to do this or what?"

"Yeah... Sorry, I'm just shy."

"I'll fix that for you." Jackie leans in and grabs Billy's face for a kiss.

"Smoky breath! Eww! Smoky breath! GROSS!" Goes through Billy's mind at first, but then his mouth becomes oddly accustomed to the harsh smoke and menthol taste of Jackie. Things begin to move smoothly with their lips.

"Shall we move to the bedroom?"

"Sure."

Jackie opens the door to her bedroom, but before Billy can close it, she is fully naked, and under her covers.

"Get naked and get under here."

"We're just going to do it? No more kissing or anything?"

"We can do it all, just get naked first."

Billy is nothing more than a piece of meat for Jackie, albeit a willing piece of meat. Billy is thrashed by Jackie. She does all of the work. Billy is essentially used as vibrator with a warm body attached to it. Jackie verbally degrades Billy and rides him so hard that he feels as though his penis might be breaking. Billy enjoys every second of the 20-second thrashing that Jackie gives to him until he prematurely ejaculates and cannot believe the events that have led up to this moment. Simple drinks to boom: the Jackie Fuck Fest!

Chapter 9

Billy is sitting in front of his desktop, working away at an account. He cannot believe the string of incredible luck that he has had so far this week. Jackie stops by his desk. She is true to her word and acts as though their sexcapade has never happened. The closest thing that Jackie does to make mention of the ordeal is her joking around that if Billy doesn't sign for the box that she is expecting the mail dude to deliver, that she will beat the crap out of him, before pausing a brief moment, and then continues with, "but you might like that." All that Billy can do is laugh nervously until Jackie walks away. He realizes that he is now scared of Jackie.

Billy looks up Frank Derico again and laughs to himself while looking at photos of the short, unevenly eyebrowed, overly tan, and overly muscular man. Derico's stature, combined with his likely steroid use, makes him too funny of a sight for Billy to handle. Billy decides that he definitely needs to see Derico in person again so that he doesn't end up laughing at Derico while waiting behind him at the bank moments before the robbery. Billy puts on a blazer and heads downtown. Billy finds a seat at the coffee shop's window that is directly facing Derico's apartment building. He sits and hopes that luck will strike twice and that Frank Derico will come out. It's still mid-morning. Billy is unsure of Derico's schedule other than he is at the club most nights and that he is usually at the bank making a deposit in the early afternoon. Billy could have waited until his lunch break for the intelligence mission, but he knew that he would be worthless at work with Derico's stature distracting his mind.

Billy's eyes catch a tall blonde woman heading north. He gives her the up and down and likes what he sees before realizing that she is walking hand in hand with a tiny yet muscular man. It's Frank Derico. Billy smiles and squirms in his seat at how tiny Derico's hand is when clasped in the grip of the tall blonde. She appears to be eastern European and is way too skinny for a normal person. At a solid six feet in height, she is likely a model. Her hand wraps itself all the way around Derico's. He looks like a little boy walking hand in hand with her. Nothing more than a seventh grader, with a soul patch, on steroids. Billy is shocked that Derico isn't with a guidette from Long Island. He zeroes in on them and tries to not find Derico funny or amusing. He needs to make the hilarity that is Derico not be funny so that the bank robbery will go smoothly. If Billy is distracted by how funny and small Derico looks, he might slip up, leave a fingerprint, or lose part of his fake face, or give away too much of his natural smile that could give the police a tip to his true identity.

Derico and the tall blonde stop outside of his apartment building as a drizzle begins to fall. Derico's gelled up, electrocuted looking, all out hair, remains slick and sharp. Not a single hair is out of place. The tall blonde leans down and gives Derico a kiss. Billy tries his best to not laugh but finds himself giggling while coyly snapping photos of the two likely lovers saying goodbye. Billy finally laughs out loud noticeably at Derico while swallowing some iced tea. It chokes him. Billy keeps snapping photos as he catches his breath. Billy plans to sit and laugh at the photos in private until he no longer finds Derico funny.

The tall blonde leans down as Derico whispers into her ear and he places a small vial of white substance in her hand. Billy suspects that it is cocaine. It reiterates something that Billy has known for a long time: MODELS LOVE COCAINE. Derico and the tall blonde finish saying goodbye. The tall blonde goes into Derico's apartment building and Derico begins to cross Park Avenue. Billy hastily puts his blazer back on, grabs his iced tea and begins to follow Derico.

After crossing Park Avenue, Derico walks south. Billy finds that is it easy to keep pace with Derico, since Derico's legs are so tiny and

Derico's overly muscular back appears to make him have a lot more wind resistance. Billy is giddy at Derico's comical walk and makes sure to keep himself between 50 and 100 feet back. Billy thinks about how one of the beautiful things about New York City is that it's a city where people are always in a hurry to get someplace, so much so, that they don't ever look behind themselves to see who is in the crowd. In a smaller city, Billy could never get away with walking block after block and following someone like this.

Derico turns right at the northern edge of Union Square and walks into the large bookstore at the northern end of the park. Billy walks through the doors and spots Derico on the escalator as he heads up to the second floor. Derico's hand is at four fifths his height while holding onto the escalator rail. Billy quickly snaps a photo of Derico looking ridiculously small in a normal sized world. Derico stops off on the second floor and begins to browse the magazine section. Derico isn't the type of person who has the will, let alone the desire, to read an entire book. Billy sits at a table within the bookstore's cafe section and watches Derico as he stands on his tiptoes to look at the magazines on the top row of the racks. Billy snorts as he tries to hold in the laughter caused from Derico parading down the aisle on his tiptoes as if he is wearing a magical pair of invisible high heels. Billy uses his cell phone camera to record a video of Derico parading around on his tiptoes. As Billy records he begins to doubt that he will ever be able to get the comical look that Derico has about himself out of the laughter portion of his brain.

Once he finishes perusing the selection of fitness magazines Derico takes the escalator down to the first floor and exits the bookstore. Billy continues the pursuit. Frank Derico heads west, crossing over Broadway and walks into a clothing store at the corner of 5th Avenue. Derico touches shirts as he walks through the store, he enjoys feeling how soft they are. Billy then enters the store with his cell phone in hand. He begins to record Derico once again while Derico holds up the shortest pair of pants that the store carries. Derico's attitude appears to change while holding the pants up against his stumpy legs. He puts the pants down and paces quickly from rack to rack as Billy tries to blend in as a fellow shopper. Derico suddenly walks directly towards Billy. Billy realizes that Derico is coming straight for him and attempts to make it look as though he is looking at a lightweight autumn jacket, but his face has a guilty look on it.

"Are you following me, bro?" Derico says with a snort.

Billy is pleased with the horrifically thick Long Island accent that Derico has. He finds it to be hysterically funny and gets himself to not laugh by concentrating on trying to bury his toes deep into the bottom of his shoes while biting on the inside of his cheeks.

"No, I'm not following you. How dare you think that I would ever do such a thing." Billy says out of the left side of his mouth.

"Buddy, I saw you in the magazine store watching me with a creepy smile on your face."

"The magazine store? You must have me mistaken for someone else."

"Are you serious? I saw you with my own eyes. Maybe you're gay or something and are into me for my muscles. Listen, I'm flattered buddy, but I'm not gay. Sexually speaking, I like women. I'm not gay, so stop following me."

Derico's "you must be gay for following me" attitude and assurances that he indeed enjoys sexual activities with women strikes Billy as an odd thing to say to someone when you think that you are being followed by them. Billy instantly believes that Derico is a closeted gay man and begins to feel bad for him. Derico is so short that most men will only find him comical and not sexually arousing. No matter how hard he tries, Derico's overcompensating muscular build will never grow his height.

"Okay. I was following you, but not because I want you or anything like that. I saw you kissing a beautiful tall blonde and I wanted to try and see if I could observe you. I thought that I might be able to pick up your swagger. Your mojo, your whatever you want to call it, so that maybe I could land a girl like you have."

Derico smirks and begins to laugh out loud to the point that Billy now knows that Derico is high on coke.

"Really guy? Just be yourself. Be sure to work out, wear tight clothes, get your eyebrows waxed, tan, and grow some facial hair. Doing all that will give you the confidence that you need and women will fall all over you. That's all that I can say about getting women. Now stop following me."

"I'm sorry to bother you man, I didn't mean to annoy you, or disturb you in any way. Thank you for giving me tips on how to pick up women. I'll try them out."

Billy begins to walk towards the door with his cell phone in hand. It is still recording. Billy realizes that he now has plenty of material to get himself to stop finding Derico funny. He just needs to watch it repeatedly to numb himself to the humor of it all.

"And buddy, if you ever manage to get a girl, always remember this: two fingers in the front and one in the back."

Billy walks out onto 5th Avenue and is barely able to contain his laughter over how awful of a human being Frank Derico has made himself out to be. Billy hails a cab and gets back to his office before noon. Billy goes back to the task of looking at suspicious activity in various bank accounts. He checks Derico's account later in the afternoon and sees that Derico made a $15,000 cash deposit shortly after 1:30PM. Derico is on a reliable schedule. Billy looks forward to Monday afternoon.

Chapter 10

A group of the under 30-something crowd from Billy's job decide that they need a happy hour outing. They invite Billy to join them. It is Billy's first invite from this crowd and comes only after his recent drinking escapades have made him into something of a legend at the office. Billy, Dean, Brian and Dustin are the last of a crowd that originally numbered about a dozen. The happy hour lasts through dinner and the guys linger around with one last drink before calling it a night. They finally call it quits and leave the Pot at around 10PM, Dustin and Brian head to their respective homes out on Long Island while Billy and Dean go to the Farm where Mia is tending bar.

"Dude, I didn't know you had a girlfriend." Dean says in disbelief.

"Yeah... well, we don't have an exact label as to what we are, so I didn't want to make any mention of her."

A drunk Dean is the true Dean. Unlike Billy, whatever is in Dean's mind and should be locked in a safe somewhere gets spilled out the more that he drinks. Dean drinks like there is no tomorrow. While it is safe to say that Billy is a mess of a drunk, Dean is ten times more of a mess of a drunk. Together they are one heck of a sloppy mess while drunk. They drunkenly opt to take the subway to the Farm and are lost underground for 30 minutes, before finally staggering into the bar where a poetry slam is going on.

"Which one is your girlfriend?"

"Right there, Mia!"

Billy's arrival signals Mia to give herself an early quitting time. Mia stops tending bar and leaves her partner Basil back behind the bar by himself. Dean is floored at the sight of Mia. He is shocked that Billy would have a hot Columbian girlfriend, with a nose ring, and a large moose tattoo on her arm. Dean's wife, Brooke, soon joins them at the Farm. Dean and Brooke are college sweethearts, who met back at Arizona State and got married too young. Being of the party school mentality, Dean and Brooke can drink without giving a second thought that maybe a 12th beer isn't a good thing.

The four of them take refuge on the corner of the bar while the poetry slam finishes up. Dean is to Billy's right, Mia to Dean's right and Brooke is to Billy's left. Billy hates poetry and poetry slams. He finds poetry to be pretentious. Thanks to the booze, Billy and Dean are being vocal between themselves about their distaste for poetry slams. They are being obnoxious jerks without realizing it for about five minutes, at which point Mia, a poet herself, finally gets them off of hating poetry as a topic.

Billy and Brooke converse and drift off into a world where only the two of them exist, despite their significant others being to Billy's immediate right. Billy is now too drunk to follow or hear what Brooke is saying, so he smiles and nods as her leg leans up against his, in what feels like more than a mere casual brush up against one another sort of thing. Billy gets the feeling that Brooke wants to have sex with him, but writes it off as the alcohol playing tricks on him.

"Billy, I need to talk to you in private right now." Mia says, interrupting the Billy-Brooke universe, as she suddenly whisks Billy off of the bar stool, and into a corner, away from everyone else, where she continues, "I think that your work friend is trying to put the moves on me."

"Get out of here. Dean is married and his wife is sitting right there."

"Well, he's being very smarmy and started being a little touchy feely on my arm. It was very inappropriate."

"I'm sure he meant nothing by it and that he is simply drunk. I won't let anything happen again."

Billy and Mia go back to the bar and before they know it 2:00AM is upon them. Billy, Dean and Brooke all need to be up for work in a few hours. Billy realizes that after nearly seven hours of downing beers, they should all go home, but the bartender, Basil, decides that it is time for an instant happy hour.

"ONE DOLLAR SHOTS!" Basil shouts.

Despite already being at the door, only one step away from the sidewalk when it is shouted, they all immediately turn around and head back to the bar. Who are they to not get happy during a late night happy hour? Dean buys multiple shots for them. Other random people who happen to be at the bar also buy them shots. As Billy and his group get three feet away from the bar, heading towards the door once again, Basil runs out from behind the bar and gives Billy one last shot on the house. Billy doesn't have any brain capacity left to realize that the seven hours of drinking and then doing a bunch of shots in less than five minutes has made him extremely drunk. Billy is so drunk that he begins to go in and out of blacking out. He cannot say goodnight to Dean and Brooke. Billy wants to take a cab home but is out of cash. He has spent it all on alcohol. Billy goes to an ATM and realizes that he has lost his wallet along the way.   The late night subway, with all of its detours and shuttle trains, is what will have to get Billy and Mia home.

Billy and Mia get on the subway and sit in a two-seater. Billy puts his legs up on Mia's and passes out on her right shoulder. At 36th Street, they have to get off and transfer for an R train to take them the rest of the way to Bay Ridge.

"Bleau? WHA!? Off?" Billy blurts out, as Mia wakes him up for the transfer. Billy slowly steps off the train. It takes every last bit of energy for him to exit the train. Billy is now on the platform. He is exhausted, so he leans against a steel support column and slowly slides down it, to the point that his body is now strewn across the platform, with only his head being upright and against the column. Billy's eyes make out a friend of his.

"It's Doobie. Look. It's Doobie." Billy mumbles, while pointing Mia's attention to his friend, Doobie, who is very noticeable, even in a crowd exiting the subway, thanks to his long beard and an Amish styled hat.

"I see that Billy is drunk again." Doobie says, with a smile, as he leans down and continues, "Would you like a Cheeto?"

"Yes." Billy's mouth starts chewing emptiness, while his hand goes into the bag to pick out a Cheeto. Billy blacks out while eating the Cheeto, Mia has to pull and tug Billy up off of the subway platform, on and off of the train, up the subway stairs, the block to Billy's apartment, and after fumbling around with Billy's keys, she finally gets them into Billy's place and into his bed.

The next morning Billy wakes up from his alarm and finds that he isn't his usual self. Normally, on the morning after drinks, Billy feels light and shows no effect of the alcohol in his system. Today, however, he is still drunk. Billy has only slept off a few of the shots. He is unable to keep his head up and is still slurring his speech. Billy realizes that he can't go into work wasted like this. He is pretty sure that he will get fired if he goes into work this drunk. Billy goes back to sleep, reawakes at 9AM and calls into work.

"Jackie, it's Bill. I can't come in today."

"Okay, Bill. Feel better."

Dustin happens to be at Jackie's desk when Billy makes this call and asks to speak to Bill.

"Bill! It's Dustin. You seemed fine when I left last night. How could you be too sick to come in today?"

"I was fine when you left, but then Dean and I thought it would be a good idea to go out to my girlfriend's bar."

"Oh dude, I feel you. Rest it off."

It is Jackie's job to tell the people who depend on Billy's reports that he will not be in and that Billy has in fact called out sick, but Jackie gets distracted by a conversation with Dustin and doesn't tell Billy's boss Chris about this phone call. Billy doesn't know this as he flops back onto his bed and curls back up with Mia. He passes out again and awakes from his phone ringing repeatedly at 10:30AM.

"Hello?"

"Bill. It's Chris. I walked by your desk and you weren't there. You're usually in the office nice and early. Are you okay?" Chris always does a visual morning headcount of his employees to make sure that they are actually at their desks and working. Billy knows this and always makes sure to be at his desk until Chris walks past on his morning headcount.

"Chris, I'm not going to lie to you. Last night I got beat up."

"Oh my God! That's terrible. What happened? Did you file a police report or have to go to the hospital?"

"No. No... I didn't get into a fight last night. I went out and the night of drinking beat me up. I called in sick to Jackie to let you know."

Billy immediately regrets telling Chris the truth and wonders why he couldn't have thought up a lie to tell Chris instead. Chris laughs and tells Billy to rest up. Billy flops back into bed once again and wakes up several hours later to the phone ringing yet again.

"You have to be kidding me. It's not even one o'clock yet. Who's calling?" Billy grumbles, as he moves to answer the phone.

"Bill? Oh man, I'm sorry man. I didn't think that I'd be waking you just now." Dustin says sheepishly.

"Don't worry about it. What's up?"

"I was calling to see how you were feeling and to apologize for distracting Jackie to the point where she forgot to tell Chris that you called in. Chris said that you told him you were beat up from the night before."

"Yeah, well that just sort of came out of my mouth. I probably shouldn't have said that, but I was feeling like death and the truth came out."

Billy hears laughter on the far end of the phone and realizes that he is on speakerphone. Everyone from Dustin's department is crowded around his cube to hear Billy's drunken stupor. What should have been a private matter, has in a few short hours, become notorious, and the biggest gossip on the 43rd floor. It's a bigger piece of gossip than Billy's drunken Christmas party shenanigans, and it is now feeding the legend of Billy's drinking abilities among the corporate casual of their office.

"Dude, what did you and Dean do last night? Dean came in shitfaced. I tried telling him that he should go home sick but he won't listen."

"Holy crap he went in. I don't how he is able to do it."

Dustin then tells Billy about how Dean arrived at work drunk, unshowered and then proceeded to go into a meeting with his manager and the bank's General Counsel. Dean was slurring his way through the meeting until he realized that he was slurring, so he stopped talking, sat down, and waved off his own presence. After the meeting, Dean found Dustin to see where Billy was hiding his drunk self. Dustin tells Billy that he couldn't stand within ten feet of Dean without wanting to vomit from the sweaty mix of booze that was coming out of Dean's pores.

When Billy hangs up with Dustin, he tells himself that he will never let himself get that drunk again. He spends the rest of the day with Mia watching her favorite movie, The Sound of Music. The singing in the movie pierces Billy's ears. As Mia leaves for a bartending shift at five, Billy is happy to no longer hear the songs. He now has peace and quiet to start his weekend.

Chapter 11

It's Friday night and Billy is restless. He hasn't left his apartment at all today and has been sitting alone in his apartment for four hours. He quickly becomes bored with television, so he counts and recounts all of the stolen cash from his bank robberies. Billy is miscalculating his counts. His first count gave him $246,980 and his second count gave him $247,020. This $40 difference is driving Billy insane, so he recounts the cash again and again. Both of these last two counts come up with the sum of $247,020. The cash has a scent. It's a dirty smell that still now has a hint of the old lady perfume scent on it. Billy packs all of the cash up and drops it beneath the floorboards of his closet. He covers it with socks, then replaces the floorboards, before finally placing his shoe rack above it all. Lastly, he places large dust bunnies beneath the shoe rack, so that there is no hint of something special, shoe or otherwise, in the closet.

Billy orders in Chinese food. He eats the General Tso's chicken and sweats. He knows that he cannot stay inside all night. The walls are closing in on him. He also knows that he doesn't want to meet up with Mia. Though he would love to sleep with her tonight, he knows that if he sees her, he will lose control of himself again and get far too intoxicated. Billy knows that he needs to keep himself as together as possible, at least until after the robbery. His next hold up is merely days away and he needs his head straight.

Billy also doesn't want to hook up with some random girl, so after watching the video he made of Derico and laughing until Derico is no longer funny, he decides to meet up with his old friend Gene.

Billy and Gene go way back. They are drinking buddies from before Billy ever got sober. Gene has never sobered up. Gene doesn't think that he has a problem. Billy knows that Gene has a problem, because Gene looks a solid ten years older than Billy does, despite being the same age. Billy can see that seven nights a week of drinking is catching up with Gene.

Billy meets up with Gene a little after midnight. There isn't much fanfare or even a happy greeting among them. Gene is unlike Billy. Gene doesn't get drunk and have sex with a girl, or do something crazy the way that Billy does. Gene is a hard line alcoholic who just wants to drink and have that be it. Gene has already kept the stool he's sitting on comfortably warm for a few hours and finds Billy's presence to be just that, a presence. Gene is no happier to see Billy than he is to see some stockbroker high on cocaine trying to play darts off in the corner.

Billy feels Gene's disdain for him and still tries to make conversation. It goes nowhere. Billy feels unwelcome by Gene, so he decides to drown himself in vodka tonics for the night. Billy stays until closing , then continues to be served for an hour after closing while the bar staff unwinds and tallies up the register. Billy is finally asked to leave at 5AM. He walks around TriBeCa and ponders breaking into a loft apartment to sleep off his drinks before robbing the place. Billy mulls it over and realizes that he is not some petty thief. He is a bank robber, a professional. He decides to take the subway home.

Billy arrives home and walks through his railroad apartment, towards his bedroom, as the early morning sun peeks through the vertical blinds. Billy's tired and drunken eyes have trouble adjusting to the sunlight. As Billy walks through his unused dining room, towards the hallway, he sees the shadowy outline of an intruder come out towards him from the hallway. Billy stops in his tracks. He knows that it is impossible for the intruder to have not seen him, for the intruder stopped moving when Billy stopped moving. Billy's adrenaline rushes as he enters fight or flight mode. Billy realizes that he is too far away from the door to escape safely and assumes that the intruder will kill him if he attempts to make a run for it.

"I'm going to have to fight for my life." Billy says to himself.

Billy sees via the shadowy outline that the intruder doesn't have Billy's looted cash. Billy takes several steps towards the hallway and watches as the shadowy figure moves further out towards him. Billy lunges at the intruder in what he assumes will be a fight to the death. Billy hopes that if he cannot kill the intruder that the fight will be loud enough for neighbors to hear, and call the police, thereby saving Billy's life. As Billy lunges forward he thinks "Well, this is it." and hopes for the best. Billy promptly lands hands first, head second, against his dining room wall, and falls to the floor. Billy missed the intruder completely and now he doesn't see where the intruder went. Billy quickly gets back to his feet, turns on the light, with his fists blazing, and discovers that nobody is there. Billy wonders if he is losing his mind, because he is certain that he saw someone walk towards him from the hallway and into the dining room. Billy looks all over the apartment for an intruder, cowering in fear, and does not find anyone. Billy shuts the light off and sees the shadowy figure once again. Billy discovers that the shadowy figure is his own shadow being cast from the sunlight. Billy tried to fight himself to the death. It is as if Billy's subconscious is trying to tell him to save himself from his own self. Billy wonders if warring portions of his own subconscious are trying to kill him with false pretenses. Billy goes to his bed and sleeps restlessly until noon.

Chapter 12

Billy exits his apartment at around one in the afternoon. The bright sun feels like a lethal dose of heroin hitting his eyes. The sun is making Billy's eyes want to close and remain closed. The summer heat and humidity immediately cause Billy to perspire; his clothes stick to his body and make him feel dirty despite having just showered. The air smells of death as the scent of old garbage and human waste rises up from the pavement. Billy looks at the people talking and laughing as they sit in the cafes as he walks along 3rd Avenue before entering the local cupcake shop. He orders a red velvet cupcake and an iced tea. This is the first semblance of a breakfast that Billy is having in a long time. Billy sits at the giant window that looks out onto the corner, drinks his iced tea, eats his cupcake, and people watches. Nobody walking past the window catches Billy's interest, bland faces walk past, they are as bland as his cupcake, which he finds to be dry and unflavored. It is far from delicious. The cupcakes from this particular cupcake shop are never moist and yummy to Billy's palate, yet the store tends to almost always be crowded. The people around Billy cannot stop talking about how tasty and delicious their cupcakes are. "Philistines." Billy quietly says to himself. Billy sees that a beautiful young brunette is feeding a cupcake to her chunky toddler. He sits there, watches and wonders if he will ever be normal enough to find a soul as beautiful and as caring as this particular woman is to be the mother of his children. Billy wonders if someone so gentle and caring would be okay and cool with the fact that he robs banks for pleasure. They probably wouldn't be. Billy knows that he cannot stop robbing banks right now and wonders if it's all merely a phase that he is going through. He reasons that if some people can go through a Goth phase, then perhaps it is possible that he is going through a badass bank robber phase. Billy then glances up and out of the windows and sees a 40-something couple who are still in their goth phase and thinks, "fuck me."

As Billy goes back to watching the precious young soul feed her chunky toddler Billy grows irritated at the realization of his own shortcomings. He realizes that he will likely never find a woman that is as perfect as this delicate woman is to be his wife and the mother of his children. Billy cannot stomach eating any more of the cupcake. In part because the cupcake is too dry, but moreso because Billy got inside of his own head and now sees himself as the person that he truly is.

Billy gets up swiftly and walks out of the cupcake shop. Half of the cupcake remains atop a napkin and dozens of little red pieces of cake are scattered about the table. It is a testament of what could have been. The cupcake should have been good, moist, and worthy of cupcake awards. Billy should have been sober, dry, not a bank robber who is spinning out of control and worthy of a good woman. Just like the chef in the back of the cupcake shop, Billy needs to improve on himself. Billy realizes that his life is quickly becoming an out of control mess, which is a really difficult and damning realization to have for a man who needs to be in control at all times. Billy thinks that maybe he should give up booze and start seeing a dominatrix regularly. At least with a dominatrix he would still be in a controlled environment while not being in total control. He wonders how long $200,000 would go with a dominatrix. Would he need to buy his own collar? Or would a collar be part of the price of a dominatrix? If it's the latter, can he get an STD via collar? Billy's thoughts are rambling and incoherent, though he is unable to realize this. Billy is merely going further down on his downward spiral. He is inching closer and closer to being completely out of control and one or two steps away from his true inner psychopath personality from overexposing itself and landing him a trip to the mental hospital. Billy walks the streets and views most everyone as being happier than he is and wonders how they do it. Being truly happy is something that Billy has long forgotten how to be and no longer remembers how to attain such happiness.

Billy's wandering of the streets has led him to a small triangular park that was referred to as Pigeon Park when he was growing up, due to there not being a proper sign to state the name of the park and the fact that the park was always full of pigeons. When Billy was a kid, the park was always full of drug users, raging alcoholics, men who didn't want the psychiatric help that they needed from the Veterans hospital and a general flow of all around low life skells that Brooklyn once had a whole lot more of. Drug Addict Park was never as inviting a name as Pigeon Park was. The park has long since been cleaned up now. It's empty, with no signs of the skells that once called this park home. Billy sits in the park by himself, looks down 4th Avenue to the towering Verrazano Bridge in the not too far distance and suspects that the old regulars all must have either died off or were given a one way train ticket to Newark. Newark is full of the old New York and the Brooklyn that Billy grew up in. Billy is the only person in the park and thinks to himself how nice Pigeon Park is these days. Billy watches the pigeons walk, peck and coo. He has no realization or idea that he has grown up and become a skell who hangs out in Pigeon Park and spends his afternoon there.

Chapter 13

Billy decides to meet up with Mia for the night. She is working her usual bartending shift at the Farm until 4AM. Billy's favorite aspect about Mia being a bartender is the often times free or deeply discounted drinks that it affords him. The extra bonus is being able to gawk at Mia as she tends bar in a skimpy top and skin tight jeans. Billy doesn't care that others can see what Mia is showing off because he knows that Mia will be going home with him for the night. Billy shows up to the Farm in the ten o'clock hour and finds the unwelcome scent of vomit and bleach in the air. An amateur had been at the bar. Mia welcomes Billy with a big smile and gives him a drink. Mia asks Billy if he read the nightly special when he is halfway through his second drink. He hasn't, so he looks up and sees that there is only one special. It reads, "Basil, stop getting Mia's boyfriend drunk." This is the first time that Mia has actually referred to Billy as her boyfriend. Billy likes the title because it makes him feel appreciated, wanted and desired. Billy smiles ear to ear upon reading it as Mia leans over the bar and gives him a big wet kiss. Mia smells like whiskey and Billy loves it.

Billy sits quietly at the bar watching the time pass. As the clock strikes midnight, Billy thinks to himself that this new day very well might be the best day of his life. He realizes that he has Mia as a girlfriend now, on top of a good job and a successful hobby of holding up banks. He wonders if maybe today will be the day that he will get his alcoholism back under control. He sits there drinking, secretly hoping that today will be the day he will clean up, or at least be the day that he can drink like a normal person, who is able to keep himself under control and not blackout. Billy takes another sip and finishes his vodka tonic just as Mia happily replaces it with a fresh one.

After the Farm closes for the night, Billy and Mia share a taxi to Brooklyn with Corey, Mia's coworker. Corey is going to a house party near Mia's Flushing Avenue apartment. Billy has done well so far with his hopes for the new day and has managed to not drink himself until blacking out. Billy is done and exhausted from the night. He wants to curl up with Mia and get some sleep. Mia knows this, but she is not ready to call it a night. She wants to keep the party going and asks Billy if he would mind it if she accompanies Corey to the house party. Billy doesn't want to go to the party, so that he can keep himself from blacking out, and hopefully begin a trend of drinking more responsibly. Billy also doesn't want to ruin Mia's night, so he tells her to go have fun at the party.

Mia gives Billy the keys to her apartment so that he can crash in her bed from his own drunken exhaustion while Mia goes out to Corey's after hour party. As the taxi peels off, Billy stands on Flushing Avenue, looking up at Mia's apartment building. It's a three story building that leans heavily to the left. The building looks unsafe. Billy wonders whether or not a heavyset person being on the left side of the building would cause it to topple over and fall into the overgrown lot next door. Billy fumbles with Mia's keys until he gets in the front door. The place is a walk-up with a rickety staircase. Billy hops over the one stair, on the second set of stairs that has heavy termite damage and stands at the door to Mia's apartment. He wonders why Mia has 11 keys on her keychain since there are only two locks on her apartment door and only one on the front door to the street. The hallway smells of skunk weed and the sound of pots and pans are echoing in the staircase for no good reason. Billy thinks about how he could never live in such an apartment building himself, for it would quickly drive him into an insane fit of rage, but it will do for the night.

Billy finally gets into Mia's apartment. The scent of bad weed is not in the air and is instead replaced by old cat litter. Billy takes a moment to decide which is a worse scent and picks the bad weed as being worse. It is pitch black inside the apartment. Billy uses his cell phone to light the way, as he quietly walks through the living room. Billy does not want to wake up Stevie, Mia's roommate. Billy quietly stops in the kitchen and gets himself a glass of water before opening the door to Mia's bedroom and laying himself down on Mia's tiny bed with his legs hanging off. About an hour later, Billy's ears awake to the sounds of Corey trying to get Mia into her building's front door. The sun has already broken the horizon.

"Careful. Careful. Shhhh... you need to be quiet." Corey says, as Mia makes random loud drunken incoherent sounds, "Where is it? I know you have one. Yes!"

Billy's cell phone rings. The ringing wakes Billy up fully and he finds himself confused by his surroundings. He answers the phone. It's Corey on Mia's phone. He tells Billy that Mia is really drunk and that he can't find her keys. Billy looks on the bed next to him and sees her keys. Billy hangs up and head downstairs while Corey continues to explain the loss of keys to a phone that is no longer connected. Billy walks down the creaky staircase and is careful to avoid the steps that look as though they will break through if a fly lands on them. He hears Mia and Corey fumbling around through the door. Billy opens the door and finds Corey giggling with a highly intoxicated Mia propped up with her arm slung over Corey's shoulders. Corey, being an extremely petite man, is barely able to keep Mia upright.

"She's a little drunk." Corey tells Billy, as he hands Mia over to him, "I have a taxi waiting who's already annoyed by us, so I need to run."

Billy helps Mia up the stairs and lays her out across the bed before fetching her some water. When Billy returns a mere 30 seconds later he finds that Mia is passed out and sweating heavily. Billy takes off Mia's shoes and a hat that she stole from the house party. Billy then curls up beside Mia on the tiny bed and falls fast asleep once again. Sometime later, Billy awakes to the sounds of Mia stumbling out of bed. Billy's initial glance makes it appear as though Mia is on the floor and stuck somehow.

"Do you need help?"

Billy's eyes finally focus and he sees the horror: Mia is completely naked and sprawled across the floor with her hands and feet in the crab walk position that little kids do during races at summer camp.

Mia's legs are spread far apart and are facing away from Billy. Billy hears something odd and gets slightly closer to see what is happening.

"Mia?"

Mia turns, although she is blacked out, looks at Billy right in the eyes and says, "Fuck you."

"Are you? Are you peeing on the floor?"

"Fuck you. Go fuck yourself." Mia continues, as she creates a large puddle of whiskey scented pee on the floor, directly between the doorway and her bed, which is frameless and sitting on the floor.

"You are! It's going to get soaked up in your bed."

"Fuck you!"

Mia finishes, and then falls on her side, next to her puddle of pee. She gets up and flops back onto the bed. Billy looks over the side of the bed and sees the huge puddle of pee. He is disgusted. Billy doesn't have it in him to pretend that he didn't see what he has just seen. Billy desperately wants to deny the realization of what has just happened before his eyes, but not even all the denial in the world can erase it from his memory. Billy is in no mood to clean the pee up, so he flops back down on the bed and looks over the edge of the bed at the puddle and watches as it continues to expand. He proclaims it to be Lake Mia before he drifts back to sleep. Billy once again reawakens only a few minutes later. Mia is pushing Billy off of the bed and towards Lake Mia.

"What are you doing? Why are you pushing me?"

"Fuck you!"

"Do you even know who I am?"

"You're my boyfriend." Mia happily replies with a smile, while wrapping her arms around Billy momentarily, before starting to push him off of the bed yet again.

"Then can you stop pushing me off the bed?"

"Fuck you!"

Billy is in a no win battle since Mia is completely blacked out. Billy gets up and carefully puts his clothes on while standing next to Lake Mia. He then has a momentary lapse in memory and walks barefoot through Lake Mia. Billy is demoralized. He quietly walks through the kitchen and through the living room, leaving a trail of pee footprints in his wake. Billy gets to the bathroom, sits on the edge of the tub and washes his feet off in the shower. He then moves to the living room and puts his shoes on. While tying his shoes, Billy discovers that Mia's roommate, Stevie, is awake in the second bedroom.

"Yo, B! Happy Sunday! What's going on?" Stevie shouts from beneath a sheet.

Billy looks over at Stevie. His eyes instantly admire her. Stevie looks so beautiful all wrapped up in a sheet on her bed. Billy quietly wonders what would have become had he hooked up with Stevie instead of Mia and realizes that he'd probably be in a similar situation.

"Happy Sunday Stevie."

"You okay?"

"Mia's being mean to me, so I'm leaving."

"Come to my bed, get under my sheet and tell me about it."

Stevie doesn't know that Mia proclaimed Billy to be her boyfriend last night. Billy stumbles with his words. He is shocked that Stevie has invited him into her bed and is unsure of what to say about Lake Mia.

"I already have my shoes on. I'll ruin your sheets."

Stevie flips the sheet off of herself, revealing her small A-cup breasts and alabaster skin that compliments her natural red hair.

"Take your shoes off and come here."

Billy is too weak of a man to say no. He tells himself that he is simply weak because of Stevie's red hair. Red hair is Billy's kryptonite. Billy quickly takes his shoes off as Stevie unbuckles his pants. Stevie takes Billy in her mouth. She makes sure that he is fully at attention for her before she takes him in between the sheets with her. Stevie is loud when Billy uses his mouth on her, but Mia is passed out and in a blackout, so she does not hear them as they go at it with the door wide open. Billy finishes quickly. He barely had three thrusts before it happened and it leaves Stevie wondering if this is normal for him. Billy gets dressed and Stevie walks him to the door. She gives him a kiss goodbye.

Mia wakes up in the early afternoon and finds Billy nowhere in sight. Mia is confused and doesn't remember seeing Billy leave her apartment. Stevie tells Mia that Billy had left earlier because she was being mean to him. She has no idea what she could have done and calls Billy up immediately. Billy tells her about Lake Mia and leaves the whole loudly screwing Stevie out of the conversation. Mia doesn't believe Billy's story of her morning acrobatic peeing or pushing festivities, so he urges her to feel the bottom of her mattress that rests on the floor. Mia feels that the mattress is soaked and knows that Billy is telling the truth about Lake Mia. She wants to vomit from disgust.

Chapter 14

When Billy hangs up with Mia, he notices that he has a missed call. He doesn't recognize the number, though it has previously been saved to Billy's phone. The name attached to the number is coming up as "Jen Bar", which means that he met her at some point recently, at a random bar, though he doesn't know where. Billy understands that Jen must have been attractive when they met for him to have exchanged numbers with her. Billy returns Jen Bar's call. She sounds cute and is being forward in trying to see if Billy would like to take her out. Billy suggests meeting at Columbus Circle and going for a walk in Central Park. Jen jumps at the chance and they agree to meet at three.

Billy gets into the shower to clean himself and ends up crying his eyes out. He realizes that his life keeps getting further out of control and that he shouldn't have allowed himself to fall off the wagon. He spends several minutes letting the hot water fall upon his head as he tries to find a way to put the blame all on Mia, but he can't find a legitimate reason to. Billy's need for sobriety, his falling off of the wagon and the blame of it all, rests solely on Billy's own shoulders and he knows it. Billy turns the hot water off and leaves the cold water on. The water feels freezing and it allows Billy to pull himself together. He steps out of the shower, dries himself off and then layers himself in deodorant and baby powder. Billy puts on a light seersucker suit and looks in the mirror. It fits his svelte frame perfectly. He then heads to the subway.

The morning fog that had earlier blanketed Bay Ridge has now been burned off and Billy needs to squint from the sun as he walks. As Billy waits for the light to change at the corner opposite of the subway entrance, he sees Kenny Gravano walking up the side street. Billy and Kenny grew up together. They were in the same grade, same classes and even played little league together. Kenny is currently strung out on drugs. His eyes are dilated and his skin has a yellowish green tint to it. Kenny doesn't recognize Billy. He's so strung out that he wouldn't recognize himself if he stood before a mirror. Billy takes a solid look at Kenny and realizes that he should stop feeling so sorry for himself. Kenny is in far worse shape than Billy is. Kenny's sight makes Billy realize that he cannot let himself slip further down on the downward spiral that he has been on recently, but stopping one's own slide down the dark path isn't as easy as it sounds. One's own willpower is usually no match to stop the dark side due to its addictive tendencies. It takes a lot to pull oneself together and Billy knows this from when he sobered himself up the first time. The red light changes to green. Billy crosses 93rd Street as Kenny turns left onto 4th Avenue, continuing through the haze of what Billy highly suspects is a heroin high.

Billy is several minutes early and pops a couple of mints into his mouth as he exits the subway at Columbus Circle. He's walking towards the big statue at the edge of Central Park. He doesn't know who he is meeting or what Jen Bar even looks like. Billy hopes that a face will pop out of the crowd or that Jen Bar will recognize him. Billy makes eye contact with half a dozen beautiful women as the walk into the park with hopes of recognizing a face. Their faces aren't jarring anything inside of Billy's head. He feels like a creep by making such eye contact with random ladies at the park, so Billy stops trying to pick Jen Bar out from the crowd. Billy sees that there aren't any other young white men sitting solo in the area, so he assumes that Jen Bar will be able to pick him out of the crowd.

"Hey, Bill Hansen! I'm digging the seersucker. It's good to see you again." Billy takes note that Jen addressed him as Bill, not Billy, so Billy knows that he must have met her at some point while out with coworkers this week. He realizes once again that he must have had too much to drink this week in order for him to not remember a woman as beautiful as Jen Bar.

"Hi, Jen Bar!" Billy says, as he greets her with a smile. "I'm sorry about the bar part. I have you in my phone as Jen Bar, and that just sounds terrible right now, because I should have had your name saved in my phone as "Beautiful Jen."

Jen smiles and laughs, "It's okay. My last name is Sullivan. Give me your phone."

Billy hands Jen his phone. He watches and worries as she scrolls through his phone and types. Jen hands the phone back to Billy and he sees that Jen's name is now changed to "Beautiful Jen Sullivan." Jen then takes her own phone out and shows Billy how he is saved in her phone "Cute & Funny Bill Hansen."

Billy is pleasantly surprised with how beautiful Jen is. Sometimes Billy's beer goggles have let him down, but that is definitely not the case here. Jen is unlike the rest of the women that Billy has seen of late. Jen is well put together. She's a graduate of Cornell, in her early 30s, with short, light brown hair, fair skin, hazel eyes and an inviting smile on top of a body that stands approximately 5' 7" tall. She is also fairly fit, but has a tiny bit of baby fat around her belly button, which Billy always finds irresistible on women.

"I'm sorry. I'm just sitting here." Billy gets up and gives Jen a hug hello, "It's good to see you too." Jen's perfume invades Billy's lungs as they hug and the scent causes him to melt inside. His eyes are glassing over as his smile remains. Billy is quickly falling for Jen.

Billy extends his right arm out for Jen to take. Jen happily accepts the offer and slides her arm around Billy's as they enter Central Park. The park is full of people enjoying a beautiful Sunday afternoon in the late summer. Jen and Billy talk as they stroll through the longest and least populated paths of the park. Hand in hand, together, they walk the edge of the lakes, ponds, and the wooded dirt paths in the hills. Billy and Jen get along swimmingly and with the greatest of ease. Billy is surprised and taken aback. He had begun to think that he had forgotten how to converse with well rounded women while sober. They talk about how they spent their childhoods, their last vacations and where they want to go on vacation to next. Surprisingly, they both have the desire to visit Germany next.

As they pass under a stone arch along a foot path in the hills near the center of the park, which is about as approximate to the center of Manhattan as a whole, Billy and Jen stop. Billy and Jen are wearing smiles that have not gone away since they met earlier in the day. The few random people that have passed them along the quiet paths have taken note with how in love they look with one another. They stand there beneath the arch, smiling, and inch ever so slowly closer. The electricity between them gets stronger with each passing inch, until their lips finally touch. They kiss, and sparks fly. Jen stops momentarily and pulls her head back.

"Bill, you're a great kisser. You're electric."

Billy pulls Jen back to him and they have a full on passionate make out session. It is so full of passion and lust that Jen gets weak in all of her joints. She drops her purse to the dirt pathway from being so weak in the heat of the moment. Billy picks the purse up for Jen and they decide to find a quiet grassy spot in the park to continue their making out. A little grassy oasis on the slope of a hill that is surrounded by trees is where they choose to lay down, close to one another, and lock lips once again. Jen wraps her top leg around Billy's. He happily accepts Jen's leg by holding it at the thigh and caresses it up and down. This make out session is hot and heavy. Billy and Jen are both in heaven. Billy cannot believe his luck. Billy feels Jen quiver and the heat that is radiating from her sweet spot when he inches high up and in on Jen's thigh. Jen is breathless, but manages to get one sentence out while Billy nibbles on her neck.

"Come back to my place. Please."

Billy happily accepts Jen's invite. He stands up and helps Jen up. Billy realizes that he has a bulging hard-on in his pants. He tries to conceal it by kicking out his right leg to no avail. Billy knows that he needs to hand adjust his crotch but does not know how to do it coyly in front of Jen. Jen spots the bulge in Billy's pants and grabs it with her left hand. Her fingers are at the bottom with her hand cupped up along Billy's shaft. Billy lets out a moan of ecstasy.

"You need to hide this until we get to my apartment. It's on 103rd, right off of Central Park West."

Billy reaches inside of his pants and adjusts himself so that his third leg isn't so prominent. They walk northwest along the crowded paths with one thing in mind: get to Jen's apartment and rip each other's clothes off.

Chapter 15

As Billy and Jen are halfway to the edge of the park, Billy's eye catches someone. It's Nancy Jacobson. That Nancy Jacobson. The one who was the bank teller in his last hold up. Billy goes cold and limp at the sight of Nancy. Nancy makes eye contact with Billy and he wonders if she recognizes him. Jen feels the change in Billy's demeanor.

"Do you know that lady?"

"Yeah, that's Nancy Jacobson. We work together. Different offices though."

Jen assumes that since Billy grew cold immediately on first sight that he must have slept with Nancy and that it ended awkwardly but she doesn't press the issue. Jen doesn't want to ruin the beautiful afternoon that she hopes to continue with Billy. She stops Billy in the path and pulls his face down for a kiss. They make out in the middle of the bridle path as a Polish tourist group passes them.

"Come on, Bill. Let's get going and continue this in a few. We're almost at my place."

Jen's block is lined with pre-war walk ups. A large group of teenagers is hanging out across the street from Jen's building. They are loudly talking about who the hottest female singers are. Billy and Jen walk up to her fourth floor apartment and take their shoes off upon entry. Jen's apartment is a spacious two bedroom with a faux fireplace, a large kitchen, and gorgeous hardwood floors. Jen's second bedroom is a junk filled home office, but her actual bedroom is enormous by Manhattan standards. Billy's first glance of Jen's bedroom makes it clear to him that Jen's bedroom is a single woman's bedroom. It has a queen sized bed that sits extra high, has a perfectly laid out duvet, a ruffle skirt and at least half a dozen pillows that surround her old teddy bear. Based off of all this visual, Billy assumes that Jen has no less than 800 thread count sheets on the bed and that they are immaculately tucked, as if a hotel maid made up the bed.

Jen pours two tall glasses of water and bring them to Billy, who is sitting on her couch in the living room. They each take a slow sip of water while lustfully making eye contact with one another. As they place their glasses on the coffee table in unison, their faces get closer to one another and their lips lock with a cool wet feeling. Their tongues gyrate and swivel back and forth, as both of their hands feel as much of the other as they can, before Jen's left hand rests on Billy's shoulder and her right hand rests with a handful of his butt. Meanwhile, Billy has his right hand on the curve of Jen's lower back, while the other is beneath Jen's shirt. He is moving the back of the fingers on his left hand across Jen's cleavage. They both moan with pleasure and smile wide while taking quick breathes in between kisses. Jen arches her back, takes off her shirt, revealing a black silk bra and a heavenly amount of creamy white breasts that are elegantly tucked away. Billy goes in for his patented feel and kiss all of the cleavage that he can move. Billy uses both hands to pull the cups of Jen's bra aside in unison to expose her erect light brown nipples. Billy immediately covers her right nipple by playing with it in his fingers, while placing his mouth on Jen's left breast. Billy sucks and swirls his tongue, as he does so, Jen spreads her legs wide and wraps them around Billy's naturally thin waist. They stay in this position for several minutes until Jen suggests they move to her bedroom.

Jen places her teddy bear onto her dresser, tosses her pillow pile to the floor, pulls her duvet back and reveals her perfectly tucked 1,000 thread count sheets. Billy cannot help but fall in love with the way Jen's breasts bounce as she undoes the bed. Once Jen is done clearing the bed Billy swan dives across it. Jen jumps on the bed next to Billy and they pick up where they left off in the living

room. Billy and Jen rip the rest of their clothes off and suck and kiss
one another's best places. Jen asks Billy if he has a condom. He
does. Billy jumps off of Jen's bed and reaches into his pants pocket.
Jen stops him as he goes to open the wrapper.

"Let me see it." Billy hands Jen the wrapped condom. "A
magnum. I love it!"

Jen opens the wrapper as Billy hops back onto her bed and feels
her breasts. She tosses the wrapper to the floor. Jen places the
rolled condom in her mouth. Billy watches Jen do this and is
confused.

"You know that it's supposed to go on me before it goes in you,
right?"

Jen pushes Billy back and down to the bed. Her soft hands run
down Billy's naturally chiseled chest and well defined abs. Jen's
soft hands continue down over the patch of hair below Billy's navel
and they stop on his hard cock. Jen takes hold of Billy and goes
down with her mouth. Billy sighs as he goes deep inside of Jen's
throat. Jen comes up gasping for air. Billy looks down and sees
that he is neatly wrapped in the condom. He doesn't want to
know, or imagine, how Jen learned to do such a move, but he finds
it to be a spectacular sex skill that he has never come across until
just now. Jen takes Billy's hands and lies on her back. While Jen
goes back she spreads her legs wide and pulls Billy up to mount her.
Billy wiggles himself inside of Jen slowly. Once he feels that she is
dripping wet, he begins thrusting hard and fast.

"OH GOD, I HAVEN'T HAD IT IN EIGHT MONTHS! GIVE IT TO ME
BABY!"

Billy smiles upon hearing Jen's words. To Billy, eight months
means that Jen is practically a virgin again. Billy thrusts and digs
himself in deeply as Jen screams, moans, and pants with pleasure.
Jen's sounds are too much for Billy. He finishes thirty seconds after
getting inside of her. Billy knows that he finished way too quickly
and Jen laughs as Billy tries to explain himself, "Jen, you're so sexy.
Your bedroom talk and squeals put me over the top there. I'm
sorry. Give me a few minutes and I'll get back up for you."

"Thanks. Don't sweat it. I have never gotten off by cock anyway,
though I loved having you inside of me. You felt phenomenal, but I
don't want to wait a few minutes.   I want you to finish me off in
another way." Jen flips herself over and puts her butt up into the

air. "I want you to go down on me from behind. Will you do that for me baby?"

Billy goes face first into Jen from behind. He works his tongue, and neck, at angles that he has never used before. He tastes the wetness coming straight out of Jen. She works her fingers across her clit, knocking Billy out of the way, while moaning, and gyrating. Billy finds that he cannot breathe and quickly realizes that his neck is cramping up from the never before used angle. Between the cramping and Jen's fingers Billy's tongue is useless. He's exhausted. He just wants to pass out and sleep things off for a while.

"You're going to need to keep doing something back there so that I can finish, Bill." Jen demands, as Billy struggles to catch his breath. Billy likes that Jen is demanding in bed and slips a couple of fingers inside of her until he finds her g-spot. He flicks and massages it. Billy does this for what feels like an eternity, as Jen keeps saying, "almost there."

Billy would have given up doing this and would have assumed that he simply couldn't get Jen off if it weren't for Jen's butt bouncing continuously in the air. Jen's hips keep gyrating in a hypnotizing motion. Jen's butt is a soft white and Billy is mesmerized by it. Billy begins to rub and caress Jen's butt with his free hand as her butt continues to seduce him until he eventually slips his index finger inside it.

"God, yes! I love that."

Billy uses this green light on the back door and proceeds to poke deeper inside of Jen's rear, ever so slowly, while Jen continues to gyrate and put Billy into a trance with it. Both of Billy's hands are doing what his tongue and cock couldn't. Jen keeps building herself up until she finally reaches the point of no return. Jen screams with joy for a solid 20 seconds. Halfway through Jen's 20 second orgasm, Billy takes his fingers out of her but he continues to watch as Jen's hips keep gyrating and are now uncontrollable. Billy smiles and tries to hold Jen's hips to share in her moment as she screams and pants in an attempt to catch her breath.

Chapter 16

The warm late summer sun is setting when Billy walks into his apartment and finds his cats curled up on the couch. He smells the three fingers that he used to massage Jen's g-spot and can still find a hint of her scent on them despite having washed his hands twice. He smiles in amazement and thinks about how his life keeps taking some of the best and worst turns of late. Billy checks his phone and sees that there are 11 missed calls from Mia that have been spread out over the course of the afternoon. Billy checks the voicemails and discovers that Mia wants to meet up with him to apologize about how she treated him earlier in the morning when she was drunk and blacked out.

Billy calls Mia up and tells her that he forgives her and that he can't see her tonight because he needs to finally get in a good night of sleep for the start of the workweek. Mia knows that Billy burned the candle at both ends a lot last week, so she accepts Billy's excuse to not meet up. Billy is now free to prepare for the bank robbery tomorrow afternoon, where he plans on taking Frank Derico's $40,000 cash deposit.

Billy proceeds to get his man-purse ready for the robbery. Billy places his man-purse on the coffee table, takes out a couple of burner cell phones, his sunglasses, retractable keychain, prosthetics, glue, a bucket hat, and the round bandages for his fingertips. Billy always places everything that he needs for a hold up on the coffee table so that he can literally see that he has everything that he will need for a smooth and successful robbery. Billy picks up his prosthetics and cleans off the old glue from his last hold up. He uses the end of a flathead screwdriver to take the chunks of old glue off. He then uses a mix of soap and water to remove the last remaining traces of glue. Billy takes his time with the cleaning to make sure that it is done correctly. The prosthetics need to be clean and smooth on the inside in order to get a perfect fit. He wants to minimize the chance with his prosthetics falling off due to old glue getting in the way of a proper fit. Billy knows that without the fake nose, or false chin, his face will easily be identified and tracked down to his name thanks to modern technology. Once satisfied that he has cleaned both pieces of his temporary face, Billy neatly places them next to his man-purse. Billy now turns his attention to making the note. He types up BANK ROBBERY. MANDI WHALEN I KNOW WHERE YOU LIVE. GIVE ME THE LAST FOUR CASH DEPOSITS OR I WILL FIND YOU IN THE MIDDLE OF THE NIGHT. Billy prints the statement and carefully laminates it. He then punches a hole into the laminate and attaches it the keychain that once held the note for Nancy Jacobson, which has long since been shredded, and discarded separately in a half dozen different garbage cans throughout the city. Billy places the keychain next to his prosthetic chin. Next, he picks up the glue and double checks how much is left. A little more than half a tube is there. Billy knows that it is enough glue for him to get the chin and nose safely attached to his face tomorrow. Billy's doorbell rings. He isn't expecting anyone. Billy stands up from the couch and leans his head towards the door, hoping that he will magically be able to see through the door, or at least hear people on the other side talking. Billy wonders if the cops have finally suspected him of being a serial bank robber and are looking to question him. The doorbell rings a second time.

"Who is it?"

"It's Mia!"

"Hold on one sec."

Billy quickly puts all of his hold up supplies into his man-purse and places it on the floor next to his door. He does a quick double check glance at the coffee table, making sure that he didn't leave anything incriminating out in the open before he answers the door. He didn't. Billy slowly opens the door. Mia is standing there, bouncing ever so slightly, with a sad puppy dog look on her face.

"I know that you want, need, and deserve a good night of sleep to start your week, but I just wanted to apologize in person to you. I'll make sure that you get to bed early and sleep well. I'm so sorry about last night. I had way too much to drink. I'm completely embarrassed about peeing all over the floor and trying to push you off the bed. Please forgive me."

Billy smiles, "It's okay Mia. I forgive you. Want to come in?"

"Yeah."

Billy gives Mia a hug and a kiss as she enters. Billy double locks his door, turns around, and discovers that Mia is on her knees and topless. She immediately grabs Billy's belt and begins unbuckling it.

"What are you doing?"

"I'm going to give you an apology blowjob."

"I've never had one of those."

Mia pulls Billy's pants and underwear down. Billy is immediately turned on as Mia pulls him into her mouth, but he is also nervous that Mia might taste, or smell, either Jen, or the rubber from the condom on him. It's too late for him to shower now and he figures that he shouldn't ruin a perfectly good blowjob by worrying about what may or may not still be on him from before. Billy goes with the flow and runs his fingers through Mia's beautiful black hair as she bounces her head forward and back. Billy smells his hands to get a scent of Mia. His hands are heavily scented with whiskey. Mia is still sweating out all of the whiskey from what she drank last night and early into the morning. Billy realizes that he has nothing to worry about. Mia is all whiskey and cannot smell or taste anything else. Billy finishes as Mia squeezes his balls with her left hand, while as her right index finger is ever so softly entering his butt. She swallows.

"You should sleep like a baby after that. Come, let's get you in the shower so that you're good and clean for bed."

Mia heads to the bathroom while Billy strips himself naked. Billy stops off at a mirror outside of his kitchen to check for any hickeys or scratches from either Stevie or Jen. Billy doesn't see any signs of either, so he walks into the bathroom, where he finds Mia naked and running her hands under the water to check on the temperature. Billy realizes once again how beautiful Mia is.

"Step into the shower. Let me wash you. The water is perfect."

Billy enters the shower and steps under the warm water. Mia follows. They kiss. Mia grabs the soap and lathers her hands. She begins washing everything on Billy from top to bottom. Making sure to stop and give extra special attention to certain spots on Billy. Mia then washes herself quickly and then goes back to washing a certain spot on Billy until he is visibly ready for round two. Mia hops up on the edge of the tub, braces herself against the wet walls, and tells Billy to take her. He enters and it feels awe-inspiring. It's the best feeling that Billy has had all day and he cannot believe what a day it has turned out to be. They quickly realize that their position is too awkward to continue. Mia gets down next to Billy so that she is standing in the bathtub and bends over. Billy takes Mia's hips. He goes hard and fast until Mia fakes an orgasm as Billy finishes. Billy doesn't know that Mia faked it. Mia always fakes them with him during intercourse. Mia then licks Billy clean.

"God, that was invigorating."

Mia grabs Billy by his manhood in an attempt to ensure that he stays hard, props her leg up on the edge of the tub and pulls Billy back into her. The water is running on the both of them. As Mia adjusts her arms for a better grip against the wall she accidentally hits her left arm into the head of the shower. The shower head breaks off. A hard stream of water is now gushing all over the bathtub. It is also spraying out onto the floor of the bathroom. Billy and Mia feel as though they are going to drown in the pouring water. They separate as Billy reaches back and turns the water off while Mia begins apologizing. Billy realizes that he cannot fix the shower himself. His plumbing skills do not exist. He'll have to get his landlord to do it.

Mia fetches towels from the linen closet, leaving a trail of wet footprints in her wake. After drying the both of them, Mia then takes Billy by his hand and leads him to his bed. Mia pushes Billy onto his back. Billy has never seen Mia so aggressive in bed and he loves it. Mia fluffs up Billy once again, gets on top of him, and gets him inside of her. The sensation of Billy sliding into Mia makes her quiver. Mia bounces up and down, smiling, while looking into Billy's eyes, and occasionally tossing, and teasing, her wet black hair across his face. Billy pulls out and finishes all on his stomach. Mia licks him up and tells Billy to roll onto his front. Mia mounts Billy's lower back, leans over to the night stand, reaches in, grabs a bottle of massage oil, pours some onto his back and begins to massage him. Billy has had a day that he never could have imagined and falls asleep almost instantly from the touch of Mia's hands on his back. Mia continues to rub and massage Billy for a few minutes even though he is out cold. Once Mia tires of massaging an unconscious Billy, she curls up beside him and stares up at the ceiling. Mia hasn't gone to sleep this early in three years. This is still practically her afternoon. Mia is simply happy and content to be there with Billy. She feels a sense of safety beside him.

Chapter 17

It is a few minutes before seven in the morning and Mia has been up the entire night. She tired of laying awake beside Billy at around three and decided to watch reruns on the television in the living room. Mia walks into Billy's bedroom and turns off his alarm clock. The sun is already bleeding through the blinds. Mia undresses, pulls the sheet back and begins to lick Billy on his magic stick. He awakes with a moan of ecstasy.

"Goddamn, this is the best way to walk up in the morning."

"I haven't slept yet, but I want you." Mia says, as she climbs up onto Billy and sits on his face. "Lick me good so that I'll pass out afterward."

Billy goes to town on Mia. When Mia finishes, she leaves Billy with a soaking wet chin and moustache of herself. Mia passes out as fast as Billy did the night before. Billy goes to the bathroom, washes his face in the sink, gets dressed for work, grabs his man-purse and heads out the door. As the warm sun hits Billy's face on his walk to the subway, he cannot help but laugh internally at this impromptu three day weekend. Billy feels well rested and is ready for the day to be a good one. After all, today is the day that Billy is expecting to see himself get away with his biggest hold up yet.

Billy exits the subway one stop before his usual one and walks to his office building. The city is alive and loud all around him. The blueish-green tints of his office building's windows make him see his office as if it is a giant box of algae. Billy presses and pushes against the revolving door to the lobby and enters it. The white marble lined lobby with 60 foot ceilings is perfectly quiet when compared to the other side of the revolving door. It is as if there is a mute button for the lobby, which feels cold and soulless. As he walks to the elevator bank, Billy is reminded that his real job in life is that of a soulless banker. His alcoholism and womanizing are not welcome here. Billy's reality is not welcome here.

Billy steps onto an open elevator and presses 43. Several other people enter behind Billy. Billy looks at their faces and sees defeat worn on each individual face. These are the faces of people that Billy has seen for years and has never spoken to for the simple reason that they work on different floors. These people all likely have overpriced houses in the suburbs, with large mortgages, sexless marriages, and careers that have hit a dead end. Plus, they all seem to gain another ten pounds of fat each year that Billy keeps seeing them. Billy hopes to never become like them. For Billy, these colleagues of his are the walking dead.

The elevator doors begin to close but then stops midway and reopens. The elevators in this building often do this due to lack of proper maintenance. The bank is too cheap for a decent elevator service contract. The doors finally stay closed on the fifth attempt, after Billy and another man force the doors to close all the way. The elevator sits at ground floor for ten seconds before swiftly rising into the sky. The elevator makes its first stop on the 39th floor. A woman gets out and marches toward her death by cubicle lifestyle. The elevator doors close on the first try this time. It once again begins to rise, then comes to a stop without opening, and then begins to drop, despite all of the pressed buttons being for higher floors. The elevator stops somewhere below the 39th floor, but does not open, and then rises once again. The elevator jerks side to side as if the cables are fighting one another and then falls yet again. Billy grabs hold of the brace bar at the back of the elevator and holds on for dear life as the elevator acts uncontrollably, until it finally stops and opens its doors at the 43rd floor. Billy exits and is out of breath from this near death experience. The rest of the people on the elevator remain on board. They are too ignorant, dumb, and lifeless from having their souls sucked out of them by the corporate world to even think of stepping off the elevator and waiting for a safe one to arrive.

Billy walks to his desk, logs into his computer and begins working.

Billy realizes that he has all of Friday to make up for and needs to take an extra long lunch so that he can rob the bank after Derico makes his deposit. Billy's boss, Chris, walks silently past Billy's desk at 9:30 on his usual morning employee head count. Billy grinds out his morning and closes reports on three different accounts for people living in the country on student visas whose accounts have a high volume of suspicious cash activity. Billy knows that these three account holders are likely terrorists. No student spends $130,000 a month being chauffeured to and from classes. At a quarter to one, Billy uses the bathroom, and then begins getting ready for the robbery. Billy throws his man-purse over his shoulder, heads to the elevator bank and hopes to get an elevator that isn't possessed this time around. At a mere ten feet from the doors to the elevator bank, Billy runs into his boss, Chris.

"Bill. I'm glad to have caught you. I need to see you in my office right now."

Billy can read Chris like the back of his own hand. He knows that based on Chris' tone of voice, and body language, that he is in trouble. Billy follows Chris quietly to his office.

"Take a seat Bill."

"What's up Chris? Is everything okay?"

"I'm afraid not Bill. Everything is not okay. Bill, I'm not sure what you have going on in your personal life, but it is clear to me that it is something dark and deep seeded. Whatever it is, it's spilling over into your professional endeavors."

"Last week was just an off week for me."

"LET ME FINISH." Chris sternly gives Bill a silent stare of death for a moment. "Over this last week you have made yourself out to be a drunken fool. You can't allow yourself to be that way. The bank cannot allow itself to let you be here that way. And I'll be damned if one of my guys walks around here and makes me out to be a fool by being a fool himself."

Chris sits in his chair and brings his hands up to his face. Chris' fingertips are touching one another. He sighs, "It breaks my heart to say this, but you need to go to rehab."

"No. I'm okay. Really, it was just an off week."

"Bill, you need some help, professional help."

"I've been working here for six years. I come in. I grind out my work and I make the bank look good to regulators. I had an off week. I'll be okay without rehab."

"The bank is requiring you to go to rehab, Bill."

"Can they even do that? I don't have a problem. Really, I don't. Chris, I plowed through six accounts on three individuals this morning, who are likely terrorists, and I filed the suspicious activity reports for you, and the bank, this morning. Who else can grind out work like that for you?"

"Sven, I think that you should come in here." Chris picks up his phone and hangs it up. Billy and Chris' conversation has been on speaker the entire time. Billy's brother-in-law, Sven, walks into Chris' office.

"Hey Sven."

"Don't you 'Hey Sven' me. Bill, you're putting the bank at risk with the behavior you've shown us this past week. The bank is requiring you to go to rehab. Are you on drugs?"

"There's no way in hell that I am on drugs."

"Good, because the bank is also requiring you to take a surprise drug test. It's simple. You pee into a cup. They test it for drugs. If you test positive, you're fired and out of a job. If you pass, you'll head to rehab come the 1st of the month. That's when a spot will be open for you at the treatment facility. The bank will pay for your stay there and you will still receive your normal salary. It's a standard and sweet one time deal the bank affords all of its employees. I can tell your sister that we sent you off to work out of the San Francisco office for the month if you'd like."

"Okay. When do you want me to pee?"

"Corporate security is coming up to the office in a moment or two. They will lead you down to their office where the drug test will be administered. After the test is administered, you will take the rest of the afternoon off. They will let us know whether or not you pass or fail tonight. We will notify you of the results. If you pass the test you need to come to work sober tomorrow and the rest of the days until the 1st."

A hard and steady knock bangs on the door.

"I guess that I'll go with them."

"Don't disappoint me. I might be your brother-in-law, but I'm also the head of this bank, and I will certainly fire your ass just like anyone else who steps over the line."

"Bill, good luck, I hope to see you tomorrow, and if not, I'll ship your personal effects to your home."

"So this is it?"

Chris opens the door to his office, "I'm afraid it is."

Three members of the bank's security team are standing in the hallway. All three of them are wearing cheap suits and one of them has a crooked Brooklyn mustache on his face. They allow Billy to retrieve his man-purse before bringing him down to their office in the sub-basement to administer the exam. When Billy leaves the security office, he looks at his watch, it is 1:30, it is too late for him to safely catch Derico's deposit. Billy walks up the stairs from the bland security office in the sub-basement to the soulless bank lobby. He presses hard and pushes the revolving door until he is back out in the real world. He is ready to be himself again.

Chapter 18

Billy walks away from his office building. He wants to create as much distance from it as possible. He is angry that he is being forced into rehab for substance abuse by the bank and is furious that the chosen time to inform him about this coincided with and ruined his plan to steal Derico's deposit. Billy feels betrayed by both Chris and Sven. Billy takes several deep breaths to calm himself down. He doesn't want his day to be ruined. Plus, the first of the month is next Tuesday; Billy knows that he will be able to take Derico's deposit next Monday. Billy ponders going to a movie, or a bar, but then he asks himself the almighty question, "What would Jesus do if he was a bank robber?" Billy knows what Jesus would want to do and exactly where he would want to go: where the money is. Billy stops dead in his tracks as he makes the realization that if you give a bank robber all the time in the world he will rob you completely blind. Billy powers his cell phone off. He decides to go hunting and the prey is dangerous. Billy is planning to hit up as many banks as necessary until his man-purse is full, all without doing any surveillance on them.

The humid air combined with the low dew point is making Billy's body feel as though it is in a broken and rundown sauna. Billy pops into a fast food restaurant, goes straight to the bathroom and locks himself inside. Billy writes an impromptu note: ROBBERY. GIVE LAST FOUR CASH DEPOSITS OR I BLOW THIS PLACE UP. BOMB!

Billy has no clue about making or obtaining a bomb. Billy is a pacifist at heart who dropped out of the Marines towards the end of boot camp when he was 18. The note is a complete bluff. He actually feels bad for needing to make such threats during his hold ups. He doesn't like knowing that he is creating a whole new world of fear, anxiety, and mental trauma for the tellers that he picks. The unfortunate fact of the matter is this: Billy knows that he won't get any cash without the threats, so he writes it off as all being part of the game, with the assumption that tellers know the risk level when they take the job.

The cleft chin is placed on first. Billy holds it tight against his real chin for 30 seconds. He opens and shuts his mouth several times to test it out and double check the strength of the adhesive. The chin is attached to Billy's liking. The nose goes on next. Billy has never figured out a solid way to test out the durability of the adhesive with the nose, so his tosses his head back and forth several times. He figures that if the fake nose is loose, he would be able to feel it then. Each fingertip is carefully covered with bandages, and his sunglasses and bucket hat are then carefully placed on his head. Billy takes a look in the mirror. He looks like a mannequin. He picks up all of his garbage to take with him and then wipes down both the counter and doorknob. He doesn't dare risk leaving a fingerprint.

Billy exits the restaurant and begins walking uptown towards one of his bank's branches. He enters the bank and notices the comfortable change in the air. The air within the bank is cool and dry. Billy steps onto the commercial business line. He is the only one on this line. The teller is finishing up with a client at her window. The client takes several hundred dollars in singles as he leaves the window. The teller then presses the button that signals the next person on line with a light. Billy steps forward with his man-purse open, pressing the note against the bulletproof glass. The teller is a young Hispanic woman. She reads the note and her eyes open wide. She hands Billy cash through the small opening at the bottom of the bulletproof glass. The bills are old and wrapped in rubber bands. They are clearly the last few cash deposits and are not anything that the bank had time to put a tracker or dye pack in. Billy casually places the cash into his man-purse and walks out of the bank without anyone knowing the better. During the robbery Billy noticed that the teller hit the silent alarm with her foot but he doesn't care because he was done with the money and out the door less than 15 seconds after the silent alarm was pressed. The call is still going through the dispatchers of the police department's communications unit as Billy hails a taxi. By the time the silent alarm call goes out over the air of the police radios in the field Billy will be two blocks away and heading downtown.

Billy looks into his man-purse. The ten by ten by three inch square man-purse is about a quarter full with cash. Billy knows that he isn't stopping today until his man-purse is full. Billy exits the taxi on Madison and 53rd Street. He does this so that surveillance cameras will not have a clear image of the taxi dropping him off. Billy easily blends in with the crowds of office drones on Madison Avenue before heading over to Park Avenue where his next target is.

The Park Avenue bank branch is one of the higher end branches that the bank has. It is considered to be the crown jewel of the retail bank. The look and feel of this specific branch is smoke and mirrors. Everything about this particular branch is an illusion to give off the impression that highly qualified fiduciaries work there. Billy knows that it is merely a trick that the bank is playing upon the wealthy. Billy knows that this particular bank branch doesn't usually have a lot of commercial cash deposits due to its location being more geared towards the upper crust of personal banking accounts. Billy wants to hold this particular branch up out of spite and to prove a point that he can easily take from the pinnacle of bank branches.

The bank has nobody on the commercial transaction line when Billy walks in. The commercial bank teller is chatting with the teller at the neighboring window and greets Billy with a smile as he approaches. Billy presses his note against the bulletproof glass. This teller presses the silent alarm much more coyly than the previous one and proceeds to slip wads of cash under the bulletproof glass. Billy puts the cash into his man-purse and notices that he got much less by volume than he did in the prior hold up. He turns to the teller and asks for one more. The teller slips another deposit beneath the bulletproof window and Billy is out the door before the bank robbery call reaches the police radios once again. Billy walks away free as a bird, without anyone other than the commercial teller and a few other bank employees knowing the better. Billy hops into a taxi that is letting someone out, lucks out, and makes the lights going south on Park Avenue. With that fifth deposit taken from this last branch, Billy's man-purse is now almost half full. The bag has some weight to it. Billy hopes that there aren't too many singles and fives in the bunch.

As Billy exits the taxi a few blocks north of City Hall, he knows that this will be his last hold up for the day. He walks south. The sun is beating down on Broadway. Waves of heat are rising up off of the sidewalk and are bringing with it the scent of decades old filth and squalor. The scent hits Billy's nose. He looks at the tourists walking all around him. He cannot help but wonder how dumb these people are to pay thousands of dollars to visit a city that smells like a rancid cesspool during the summer months. The nearby tourists are speaking with a touch of twang in their accents. These tourists will return home and think fondly back on their time spent in Manhattan, shopping for knock off handbags, and think of themselves as being both cultured and world traveled from their comfy couches in Tennessee for having gone to Times Square and Chinatown while smelling the feces of drugged out and mentally deranged homeless men.   Billy momentarily feels sorry for them as he walks further south.

A traffic cop stands in the middle of Chambers Street. She is holding southbound traffic while blowing her whistle for the cars to continue going east through the red light along Chambers Street. As the walk signal turns and begins to blink a red hand, the traffic cop stops the Chambers Street traffic and pulls cars southbound. This allows Billy to cross the street and be on the block of his next hold up. He stops at the curb and takes a deep breath of air while admiring the architecture of City Hall. Billy's lungs are adjusted to the bad smells and the extra deep touch of oxygen feels good to him. He turns and walks into the bank. Two people are waiting on the commercial teller's line and one man is currently at the window. Billy waits patiently and blends in with the crowd.

Billy holds the note low at the bulletproof glass when it is his turn at the window. He does this because this particular bank branch has a much smaller layout than the others that he has robbed so far today. The close quarters makes it easier for other people within the branch to notice what is happening at the teller windows. Several people within the bank notice the robbery in progress. Billy puts the cash into his man-purse in a hurry and turns for the door.

As he does this he sees that a personal banker who normally sits at a desk with the job of opening bank accounts is now charging toward him. Billy sidesteps the wannabe vigilante and uses the guy's speed and aggression against him. Billy grabs the wannabe vigilante while stepping aside and throws the man to the floor. The people on the regular line for the tellers begin to step out from behind the velvet rope. Billy throws his man-purse up under his left arm and runs for the door. Another foolish man tries to be a hero and blocks the door. Billy throws his head and shoulder down and barrels through the man. They both fall down across the floor of the ATM vestibule. Billy quickly gets up and runs out onto the street. He knows that his best chance of escape is by getting into a crowd and blending in.

City Hall and police headquarters are to his east, while the courts and central booking are to his north. Billy's routes of escape are limited. Billy lost track of time and isn't sure how much longer he stayed inside of the bank with those two guys trying to stop his escape. He knows that the silent alarm was pressed when the teller read the note and figures that it is probably only seconds or maybe even a full half minute extra, but every second counts and comes with real ramifications of prison during bank robberies. Billy runs west on Chambers Street. The fact that he had physical interaction and knocked two people to the floor will bring out a larger police presence for this robbery. As Billy runs, he realizes his shortsighted mindset is very well likely to get him caught and sent to prison.

Billy zigs and zags through the crowd of people on Chambers Street clutching his man-purse the way a running back would hold a football after they break out into an open field. The bag feels full. Billy turns right onto Church Street and runs another two blocks before beginning to walk in an attempt to blend in with a crowd of people. Billy hears the wails of sirens and sees several police cars circling. He assumes that the cops are looking for him and haven't spotted him yet. Billy knows that he isn't blending very well and doesn't want to risk crossing Canal Street since he will stick out like a sore thumb with his extremely sweaty clothes. If Billy stays on the streets it will only be a matter of time before the police spot him and pick him up. He turns right onto Walker Street.

"04, 07, 03, 03, 08" Billy mumbles to himself. That's the pin code that Billy used years ago to enter an old building on Walker Street to cat sit for a friend of a friend who lived in a big loft. He isn't sure if the building still uses the same pin code but decides to give it a shot since his options of escape are dwindling. Billy types the pin code and the door unlocks. Billy is amazed that the people of the building never thought to change the code in ten years. Billy heads down towards the original first floor of the building. The present day ground floor is actually the second floor from when the building was originally built. Decades ago, the city decided to make lower Manhattan as level as possible, so they raised the street level on many TriBeCa streets to be at the second floor of the existing buildings. This caused many exquisitely designed entryways to become hidden below the street level. Billy walks downstairs and out of the original first floor entrance. He is now one floor below the modern day street. He looks up and sees the sunlight bleeding down through the round pieces of glass that adorn the sidewalk. He looks at his watch. It's a little before three. Billy decides to wait it out down there because he knows this block like the back of his hand and can run and hide should someone come find him. The police tour change happens at four and then the sun will set a few hours after that and the streets will be nearly empty and almost unrecognizable as being those of lower Manhattan. Billy checks his face. He feels lucky to discover that his prosthetics are still attached. He begins removing them in an attempt to change his appearance. He turns a spigot of water on, washes his face and drinks from it. The time just needs to pass.

Chapter 19

The sun hasn't shown through the glass circles above Billy's head for more than an hour. Billy looks at his watch and thinks that it is about time that he begins his final escape of the day and his voyage home. His face has been cleaned. His prosthetics, sunglasses, hat and used fingertip bandages are all stuffed inside of his man-purse. There was just enough room to squeeze them all inside.

Billy doesn't want to use the way he came into the building as his way out. He cannot risk the chance that he was seen going into the building and that the police are simply waiting for him to come out of his hiding place. He tosses his man-purse over his shoulder and walks up the stairs to the roof and kicks a stone that is used as a doorstop over to prop the door open. The fresh night air feels good on Billy's face and the taste of freedom begins to run through his veins. He walks over to the roof of the neighboring attached building and checks the door with the cuff from his sleeve covering his hand. By some miracle the door is unlocked. Billy opens the door and sees total darkness. This building doesn't have a light on in the staircase. Billy assumes that it is due to the building's co-op board being too cheap to turn them on at night. The tenants all have elevator access to their giant loft apartments which span the entire length of each floor and have no reason to normally use the stairs. Billy doesn't want to risk making any of the building's tenants aware to his presence by turning the lights on, so he stands carefully at the top of the darkened stairwell and feels around until his hand catches it. The rail feels wooden, smooth, and well painted. Billy begins his quiet and dark decent to the basement of this building in hopes that what Christian drunkenly told him at the loft party last week is true. Christian grew up around the corner from this building. He claims that this building was originally built to be a storage location for a shipping company in the mid-19th Century and that a tunnel connects this building to the smaller and much older building at the corner of Church Street via the cellars. According to Christian the small building on the corner was the original shipping office at the time and the Hudson River at the time wasn't blocks away as it is now in present day. Christian claims to have played in the tunnel as a little kid, some 20 odd years ago. If the tunnel really exists and was open back then, then there's a slight chance that it still might be open tonight. Billy slowly makes his way to the original basement, which is two floors below the modern day street level. He knows that he is in the basement when he cannot feel any more stairs in the pitch black. He also can't see if the tunnel that Christian claims to exist really does exist. It's simply too dark for him to see anything. Billy feels along the wall until he finds a light switch and flips it up. The light comes on and reveals a labyrinth of old junk that is spread across the cellar. Billy walks through the maze of junk as he tries to see the walls. He doesn't see any obvious sign that there was ever a tunnel that came out of this cellar and begins to wonder if Christian's drunken story is nothing more than just that. Billy begins pulling out boxes away from the wall at random. The entire first two walls of boxes that he does this to are hiding nothing. It is on the third wall that Billy finds a primitive cut out that is approximately five feet in height and open. It is completely dark inside of the tunnel. Billy cannot see his hand when he holds it directly in front his face. He crouches and walks through the tunnel while holding onto the wall. It feels damp inside and is spooky with the sounds of rats squealing in the darkness.

Much to Billy's surprise the tunnel actually exists and the opposite end doesn't have a door or gate blocking access to it either. Christian's drunken story is true. Billy simply walks directly through the tunnel and into the cellar of the corner building. Now that he is in the basement of the corner building he still can't see where he is walking. He is walking blindly but he is fairly certain that he is the cellar since the wall made an abrupt 90 degree turn.

Billy walks slowly and bumps into several stacks of boxes in his journey through the darkness while trying to locate the staircase. When Billy reaches the western portion of the cellar, he can see the faint glimpse of streetlight coming in from Church Street. He carefully maneuvers through boxes to the base of the stairs. He looks up, and sees that light is coming through a door two landings up, so he quietly ascends the stairs, which are old, wooden, and creak with his weight on each step. Billy stops on the second landing and sees two doors opposite of each other. The door with the streetlight bleeding through its window leads to the street and the other leads to the inner part of the building. Billy places his ear up against the inner door and can hear that it is the door to a restaurant's kitchen. There is too much background noise in there for the chefs or waiters to have heard him climbing the staircase. Billy opens the door to the street and sees the rear end of an unmarked police car. He knows that it's the cops since it is a black Chevy Impala with multiple small antennas on the top of its trunk. The windows of the car are open and the car is parked facing the wrong way. It is occupied with two guys who have thick Long Island accents. Their police radios lie across their laps as they shoot the breeze and look south. The cops don't notice that Billy came out of the building and is now listening in on their conversation.

"The captain is giving this guy until midnight. If there isn't any sign of him by then, we'll get the warrant, bust the place, and find him. He's probably living in a 4,000 square foot loft and paying the rent by robbing banks. The eyewitness at the station says he saw a sweaty guy go inside. It has to be him."

Billy looks at his watch. It's a little before 11. He quietly walks north a free man. Billy makes a right onto Canal Street and hails a taxi at Broadway. He takes the cab to Brooklyn and exits it at 65th Street and 4th Avenue. The location is the underside of an elevated highway and there are no security cameras that can see his exit. Billy walks the final 25 blocks to his apartment so as to avoid any paper trail from the taxi.

As Billy opens the door to his apartment his cats run over to his legs. They rub up against him for some affection. Billy goes over to his couch and they follow. He rubs his cats behind their ears as he turns his cell phone on. There are three voicemails.

"Hey Bill, this is Chris. I got word that you passed the test. I look forward to seeing you sober tomorrow."

"Hi, this message is for William from bank security. You passed your drug test and can return to work tomorrow."

"Bill, it is Sven. I told your sister that you're going out to San Francisco for a few weeks. DON'T FUCK THIS UP!"

Billy immediately realizes that something went wrong with his drug test. Corporate security fucked up the samples. Someone else is going to be fired because of the pot cookie that he ate. He tosses his cell phone across the room and it lands on the floor. He realizes that he was much happier hiding from the police in a cellar than being connected to his work life. His cats continue to purr and enjoy his rubs as much as he is enjoying petting them. The cats eventually settle in, spread out across the couch, and fall asleep as Billy continues to pet them.

After the cats are out cold, Billy turns his attention to his man-purse full of cash. He looks at it in disgust. His own rage and the lack of planning almost got him caught today. The money feels dirty this time and Billy is dreading having to count it. He isn't even sure which bundles are from each specific branch. The cash got jumbled up inside of his man-purse during his escape. Billy holds his man-purse upside down which allows his disguise and all the cash to flop across the coffee table. He places the disguise back into the bag and then begins his count. There are a lot of small bills. Two hours later, Billy has several neat piles of cash on the table before him totaling $48,591. Billy looks over at his cats. They are content and asleep. He realizes that he's been sober for about 42 hours, and has done fairly well for himself while sober, despite having had one of the most dangerous days of his life. Billy wonders if maybe all it took to sober up was the visual of Mia peeing all over the floor of her bedroom for him to hit rock bottom. He thinks that the week should be a good and easy one to live sober.

Billy places the cash neatly below the floorboards of his bedroom closet and gets ready for bed. He lays in the dark and checks his phone one last time before he closes his eyes. There are no more calls or messages. He hasn't heard from Mia all day, but then again he didn't reach out to her either. Billy texts Mia, wishing her a good night, then turns off his phone, and lets the dreams of his subconscious take hold of him.

Chapter 20

The pile of completed suspicious activity reports has grown higher throughout the day, as Billy takes a no holds barred approach to his work today. Chris keeps delegating more suspicious accounts Billy's way. The constant glaring of light from the computer screen is making Billy's eyes become bloodshot. He hasn't heard a word from Sven or Chris today, aside from a "morning" when Chris passed on his daily head count. Most of the people on Billy's floor have left for the day, but he remains there working, until his eyelids begin to fail him and want to remain closed. A newspaper is folded up at the end of Billy's cube. His face is on the cover of it with the headline: "HUNGRY HUNGRY BANK ROBBER". Billy isn't too worried about the photo or press coverage since the photo is grainy and his costume has greatly obscured his true identity. The articles inside talk about how approximately $75,000 was taken during the robbery spree and tells of how two people suffered minor injuries and asks how the robber was able to elude capture and how both eyewitnesses and video place the robber going into, but not coming out of, a building on Walker Street.

Dean has been working late tonight as well and stops by Billy's desk.

"Happy hour?"

"Absolutely, I need it today. Look at all the work I did today." Billy points to the pile of suspicious activity reports.

Billy and Dean bar hop for several hours until Dean looks at his phone to check on the time and sees that he has a lot of missed calls.

"Holy fuck! How do I have 17 missed calls from my wife?"

Dean checks his voicemails. Dean's wife is wondering where he is since they were having a contractor coming over this particular night to discuss putting in a new kitchen in their apartment. Dean's wife sounds angrier at him with each voicemail for blowing off the appointment. "My wife is pissed at me. I should go home."

"I should too."

Dean jumps into a taxi and heads home. Billy heads to the subway with all intentions of going straight home, but when the R train reaches Prince Street Billy's urge to use the bathroom is too much. He exits the train and walks over to the Farm. Mia is behind the bar as Billy walks through the door. She smiles and blushes at the sight of Billy. They kiss over the bar and then Mia gives Billy the key to use the employee bathroom. Upon returning to the bar, Billy finds that Mia has several shots poured out on the bar.

"These are for us." Mia has a beaming smile that makes Billy melt inside. Billy is falling madly in love with Mia and knows that he shouldn't be. Mia is bad news for Billy and only helps Billy feed into his own dark demons of alcoholism, yet he finds himself wanting to run off and live with Mia on an uncharted island. He thinks that this would be bliss. Billy and Mia down the shots. Billy's world goes black. His blackout lasts several hours. He doesn't know how long he stays at the Farm or that he was even at the bar.

When Billy comes to his eyes are already open and he feels as though he has just reentered his body in a crashing manner, as if he just ended an out of body experience. He isn't aware of his surroundings or what he is doing at first. A moment passes, Billy then realizes that he is in his apartment and that he is having sex. Billy is on top of someone. He feels his soul feels lunge out of him once again, but watches and feels as it happens this time. Billy is now at the top of his bedroom. From this vantage point at the ceiling Billy sees that he is on top of Mia and then he once again crashes back into his body. Mia feels so good. Billy kisses her cheek. She doesn't move. Billy begins to wonder how they got home and how they started to have sex. Billy looks at Mia again. Billy slows down the pace of the sex. He is unsure if Mia is aware that he is inside of her. Billy looks at Mia a third time and this time he notices that Mia's eyes are rolled into the back of her head.

"I don't think that Mia's home in there right now." Billy says to himself, as he stops the sex altogether.

"Harder..." Mia whispers to his surprise. "Harder... fuck me harder."

"I guess she's awake after all." Billy's mind says with ease. Billy blacks out again and doesn't know that he finishes inside of Mia. Both Billy and Mia stay blacked out and sleep the rest of the night away. As they wake in the morning they feel extra frisky. Billy has forgotten all about those 30 seconds of being aware. Mia positions herself for some lovemaking, and when Billy enters her dragon, it all comes rushing back to him.

"Do you remember having sex last night?"

"With who?"

"With me, silly."

"We never had sex last night."

"Yes, we did. I woke up from being blacked out and we were doing it. I thought you were blacked out too, so I stopped, but then you seemed awake because you demanded that I do it harder. So we continued and then I blacked out again."

"I don't remember anything of that. We had sex?"

"We totally did."

"Well, at least I'll be able to remember how good it is this time."

Mia pulls Billy inside of her and then rolls herself on top of him. She does all of the work. Even though Billy feels great inside of her Mia fakes an orgasm per her usual and Billy is none the wiser. The fake orgasm pushes Billy over the edge and he pulls Mia off of him a split second before he finishes. His juices land on top on his stomach. Billy cleans himself up. He needs to get out and go to work. He is a two minute marathon man on the run.

Chapter 21

The central air blows a steady 70 degrees into the cubicles on the 43rd floor of Billy's office building. It's just cool enough not to be able to legitimately complain about the temperature being too hot while at the same time being too warm of a temperature to sit inside comfortably all day. Billy is on his third large iced tea before noon and is mindlessly doing his reports while on autopilot. Though Billy is actively working he is also spending his day at work thinking about Derico's cash. He's seen it with his own eyes and knows that it is the easiest load of nearly $40,000 to walk away with.   Billy does a solid ten hours of work and then heads to the Farm to meet Mia for drinks on her off night.

   Mia is much later than her norm to meet Billy and when she arrives at the Farm he discovers that she is slightly out of it. Billy chalks Mia's odd behavior up to her having lost track of time at home. He assumes that she was pre-gaming and had too many shots of whiskey before heading over to the Farm. But then Billy notices that Mia cannot sit still no matter how hard she tries. Mia suggests that they go for a walk. They walk three blocks north before deciding to sit on the stairs of a building on a quiet side street.

   "Billy, I need to tell you something. I'm really high right now."

   This isn't anything new. Billy always knew that Mia enjoys smoking weed, but she quit smoking cigarettes at his request, and so he figures that a couple of hits of pot every few days is better than a pack of cigarettes a day.

"Okay. You're high."

"No, you don't understand. I'm so high right now and it's great."

"What's so great about it?"

"It's this speed that I got." Mia pulls out a bag and tries passing it to Billy.

"I don't even want to touch that. Put it away."

Mia's admission to being on speed sets off another mental grenade inside of Billy's head.

"I've wanted to do more speed ever since that night at the Farm last year when you took care of me as I crashed on a chair. I was climbing the walls craving it, but now that I know that my coworker, well, my coworker Dee, his roommate is a dealer..." Mia cuts herself off as she momentarily giggles uncontrollably, "...life is going to be so much better."

Billy is stunned by this news and is trying his best to remain as calm as possible.

"Do you really want to keep doing speed?"

"Yes. It's so good. It makes everything so much better in life. I have no worries. I'm going to be doing this all the time now that I know where to get it. Life is going to be so much better from now on."

Mia holds the baggie in her hand out and offers Billy her drug of choice once again. Even if Billy wanted to try speed he wouldn't know what to do with it. He doesn't know if it's something that should be smoked or snorted.

"I seriously don't want to touch that. Please get it out of my face."

Billy's heart breaks instantly at Mia's realization that she wants to become a drug addict who gets high on speed every day and throw her life away.

"Take some. You'll love it."

"Seriously, get it out of my face."

"What's your problem?"

"You're on meth right now."

"No, it's not meth. It's speed. It's a watered down version of meth."

"It is close enough that it might as well be the same thing!"

"Well, it's not. So don't get yourself all up in arms over it. I'm not some junkie."

"I don't want to get into the semantics of this with you, and I... and I... I'm just not comfortable dating someone who does..."

"I can see that you have a problem with it." Mia throws her bag of speed towards the curb. "It's just some speed. It's not meth. I've done it before. It's no big deal."

"I wasn't comfortable with it the first time that you did speed."

"We weren't dating then."

"And we're dating now. I always told myself that if you moved onto harder drugs..." Billy sighs, "I don't know how to say this other than I really don't think that I can be with..."

Mia runs off before Billy can finish his words. She doesn't want to hear that Billy can't be with her because she wants to live a life on drugs. Billy doesn't run after Mia. Instead, he sits on the steps and is utterly stunned at the sudden implosion of his relationship with her. He looks at the bag on the sidewalk and hates it. Part of Billy wants to hunt down and kill Mia's coworker, Dee, and his roommate, for selling her the drugs. But Billy knows better than to actually do this, because it was Mia's decision to take and do the drugs. They happened to supply them. All three of them are in the wrong, but none of them deserve death for it. The night air suddenly feels like it got hotter by 20 degrees. Billy shakes his head and tries to gather his thoughts. He sits on the steps for several minutes while trying to hold himself together. Billy takes several deep breaths of air and walks toward the Farm where his half drunk beer is. Billy guesses that he and Mia just broke up but he isn't exactly sure. He knows that he doesn't want to cut off the friendship that he has with Mia, but at the same time he can't stand by and be with someone who wants to throw their life away by becoming a junkie. Billy is confused and isn't sure what to do about the situation. All he knows for sure was that he is deeply hurt by the whole thing.

As Billy walks down the street he feels as though he is floating in a haze of fog. In the distance he sees a bunch of people standing outside of the Farm. He doesn't think much of it since people almost always linger outside of the bar smoking cigarettes and chat with one another. As Billy gets closer he can hear and see that Mia is in hysterics. Tears are exploding out of Mia's eyes and are rolling down her face as she cries and hyperventilates. Several people are trying to calm Mia down and figure out what is causing her distress.

Billy makes eye contact with the woman closest to Mia. She is trying to console Mia as he walks past them and into the bar. Billy is stunned, cold as ice, and doesn't want to talk to anyone. Billy tries to drink the rest of his beer in peace but cannot because he is too distracted by Mia's wails that can be heard bleeding through the door.

"Billy, what's going on? Why is Mia so upset?" Basil asks.

"I don't want to talk about it." Billy is barely able to speak without his voice cracking and is almost to the point of tears himself.

"Well, Mia's really upset. Maybe you should try to help calm her down."

"I can't."

A short while later, Billy realizes that he feels too uncomfortable by the situation and then leaves without saying another word to anyone. He walks over to a liquor store, buys a bottle of vodka, and then catches a taxi. The driver is a middle aged Bangladeshi man who inquires about the woes of Billy. Billy proceeds to drink straight from the bottle as the driver takes him home. Billy spills his guts to the driver about how hurt he is feeling about Mia right now. The taxi driver tells Billy that if he really loves Mia, then he should help her not be a drug addict, and to live a good life. The driver also reminds Billy that he shouldn't be drinking the way that he is. As Billy pays and exits the taxi the driver gives Billy one more piece of advice, "Sleep it off. In the morning you will have a different viewpoint. Remember that the sun destroys the evils, sadness and dangers of a dark night, and tonight my friend you are having a very dark sad and dangerous night of evils. I wish you well my friend. I hope that the morning sun destroys the bad cloud that currently surrounds you."

Chapter 22

The empty soulless glare emanating from the computer screen is shining a light on Billy's pale face as a buzzing sound from the overhead florescent light periodically sounds on and off. The buzzing is slowing driving Billy mad as he works on reports. He does not want to be at work. He is grief-stricken. Billy is brokenhearted at the sudden implosion of his brief relationship with Mia, despite the fact that even he knew all along that things between he and Mia would never work out. Between the age difference and their combined substance abuse issues, a successful long term relationship would have been nearly impossible. Billy still has love for Mia nonetheless. Plus, their sexual chemistry was magnificent for Billy. He is going to miss the sex with Mia the most and knows that if missing sexual chemistry of someone is the one thing that he will miss most about them then the relationship shouldn't be. Billy reminds himself that there are plenty of fish in the sea and wonders about Janet. She flew back to California the day after they hooked up. Billy wonders what it would be like to leave everything behind in New York and start fresh in California with Janet. Billy begins to imagine what it would be like to be with Janet again while working on autopilot. He is working on his boring reports as his mind races a thousand steps a minute fantasizing about Janet's curves. He is full on using his work autopilot that has helped make him the best anti-money laundering analyst that the bank has. Billy is about to mount Janet inside his mind when the autopilot reaches out to the actual pilot. The account that Billy is looking at has recently made several highly suspicious cash deposits in Nevada. On one occasion, one Wendy Clarke deposited $38,870 in one dollar bills. Two days later, she deposited $22,300 in five dollar bills, and the day after that she deposited $17,500 in ten dollar bills. Nearly $80,000 in cash was deposited into an account that has seen sparse use in the four years that it has been open and has had an average daily balance of $2,300 for the past two years. The cash by itself isn't what piqued Billy's interest. What catches his eye is that Ms. Clarke lists her occupation as adult entertainer and that her employer is a prostitution ranch just outside Las Vegas.

A quick internet search of the Apple Bottom Ranch in Nevada takes Billy straight to a website that offers the sexual services of women. Billy clicks the link, both to print the website out for his report and to see how pretty the women are. The five women with photos are a six at best and claim to be in their mid-thirties. Ms. Clarke's bank account has her age listed at 43 and there is a Wendy listed on the Apple Bottom Ranch's website whose age is also 43. The website does not have a photo listed for her. Based off of how lacking in the beauty department the women with photos listed are Billy thinks that it's safe to assume that Ms. Clarke looks like hell. Billy's intrigue with Ms. Clarke vanishes nearly as soon as it arrived due to the lacking photo. Billy picks up his cell phone and sends a text message to an administrative assistant, Robin, who sits near Jackie. Ever since Billy slept with Jackie last week, Robin has been extra flirty with him and has even sent Billy photos of her bare chest. Billy assumes that Jackie told Robin about how she slept with him. That's the only reason for Robin's sudden overt actions. Billy sends Robin a message asking for her to send him a photo of the panties that she is wearing today. Billy's phone buzzes five minutes later. It's a message from Robin that contains a photo of her butt in the mirror of the women's restroom. Robin is wearing underwear with black and white horizontal stripes on it. Robin's butt and legs look as sexy as her bare chest did in the previous photos, especially for a woman in her mid-forties. Billy wants to forget all about Mia and sleep with Robin tonight.

"Can I take you out for a drink tonight?" Billy texts as a reply to Robin's butt.

"Yes, on one condition. You need to sneak into the women's

restroom and let me give you a blowjob in the last stall."

Upon reading the condition, Billy drops his cell phone and nearly falls out of his seat. Robin is as up front and even more blunt and kinkier than Jackie is. Billy picks up his phone to write back and sees a second message.

"I'm all alone in here. Hurry up."

The door to the women's restroom is in the hallway at the center of the 43rd floor near a small kitchen area. Billy gets up from his desk and tries his best to act as if he is walking as normal as possible but he has a grin that will not leave his face no matter how much he wipes the grin down. Billy walks past the women's bathroom door and heads to the kitchen. He opens the refrigerator and pretends to peer inside as he scopes out the hallway to see if the coast is clear. Billy takes a deep breath and heads to the women's restroom. As he is about to open to door, the handle turns, the door pulls away from him and opens. Billy jumps back and throws his back up against the wall of the hallway in a most obvious manner of suspicion. A summer intern whose name Billy never got walks out of the restroom. The intern never looks to her left to see Billy standing suspiciously. She instead turns right and leaves the hallway for the corridors that are lined with cubicles. The intern never notices Billy. He catches the door before it closes and enters the women's restroom.

Scared out of his mind and in a blind spot to most of the restroom Billy takes a quick peak around the corner to see if anyone is in there. The sink area is clear. Billy walks inside and notices a red sofa and a fancier mirror than the one that hangs in the men's room. He wonders why they are there. He wonders if women sit around on the sofa and listen to each other go about their business in the stalls or if the sofa is a waiting area for when the stalls are all occupied. Billy looks beneath the stalls and sees legs at the last stall. All of the other stalls are clear. Billy clears his throat to signal whoever is in the stall that a man is present in the women's restroom.

"Bill? Is that you?"

Billy races toward Robin's voice. She unlocks and then opens the last stall to allow Billy to get inside with her. Robin's hands go directly for Billy's crotch. Robin undoes Billy's belt, unzips his pants, and yanks them down to his knees along with his underwear.

Robin's hands hold Billy's balls as her mouth swallows his plump manhood. Robin goes to work fast on Billy. He looks down to watch Robin do her thing with a smile on her face and takes notice of her hands. Robin's hands are quite large with long and thick fingers. Other than their enormous size, they still manage to be oddly feminine in shape. Billy wonders whether or not the size of a woman's hands has any direct correlation to the size of her vagina. Someone enters the restroom.

Robin stops what she is doing to put one finger over her mouth, signaling Billy to remain quiet and then goes back to town on him. The mystery woman flushes and washes up before leaving. Billy wonders about the sofa again. Is it all just for show? He suddenly grabs onto the walls. He's done. He cannot believe that he just sneaked into the women's restroom at work or that Robin just did what she did. Billy is out of breath.

"I want you to take me out for drinks and then I want you to do the same thing for me tonight."

"You want to sneak back into work and come into the women's restroom after the bar?"

"No. My place. My bed. I want you to give me your all tonight. Will you?"

"Yeah..." Billy continues to pant. "Sure. We can do that. It'll be fun."

"Good." Robin pulls Billy's pants up. Smiles. Gives him a kiss on the lips and grabs his butt with both hands. "Get back to your desk safely."

Robin leaves Billy in the stall and walks out of the restroom. Billy takes a minute to gather himself and then it hits him that he is alone in the women's restroom at work. He wonders what he was thinking to allow himself to be in such a predicament. If he gets caught he will be fired.

The stall door is slowly opened. Billy hasn't heard anyone come into the room but he is still worried. He tiptoes towards the door as if he will wake up a mouse. The door to the restroom is flung open suddenly. Billy, hearing the door open, quickly sneaks into the first stall, locks it and picks his feet up. The footsteps come closer and continue past Billy's hiding place to a stall further down. Billy hears the door to the stall lock and the sound of a protective sheet being placed onto the toilet seat. Billy unlocks the door to his stall and makes a run for it. He bolts to the door, opens it, and shoots himself out of it to the hallway. He's out of breath and sweating from fear as he makes it through to the safety of the cubicle lined corridors. Billy brushes his clothes off with his hands and walks back to his desk.

At six o'clock sharp, Billy finds Robin standing at the entryway to his cubicle.

"It's time." Robin says with a smile.

Billy and Robin go to the Pot and have two drinks. Robin wants to converse with Billy to give herself a sense that she is at least being wined and listened to before jumping into bed with him.

They hurry back to Robin's apartment and are fooling around. Robin's top is pulled down around her bellybutton and her skirt is up over her top. Only Robin's midriff is covered with clothing. Billy's mouth is all over Robin's special blonde mound. They are both in heaven. Billy keeps moaning with eager anticipation, as Robin does the same, except she also keeps saying, "Bill... Bill... Oh God, Bill." Billy begins to pet Robin's insides with his fingers and it drives Robin wild. Billy is searching for Robin's g-spot and cannot find it. He then remembers how big and long Robin's hands are which causes him to assume that there must be a direct correlation between the size of a woman's hands and the size of her vagina. Robin's vagina appears to be a spacious and cavernous land of pleasure. Billy continues to slip more fingers inside of Robin as she quivers and moans in ecstasy. Billy eventually realizes that all of his fingers are inside of Robin. Robin finds them quite enjoyable as Billy continues to flick his tongue and pucker his lips against her. Robin's body seems to want more so Billy puts his hand deeper inside of her. Billy is in unchartered territory and now has his fist inside of Robin. Everything up to his wrist is inside of Robin. Billy finally finds her g-spot and begins to massage it. It only takes about 30 seconds of Billy's massage for Robin's body to seize and for her to scream at the top of her lungs into a pillow. Robin's hips are writhing as she wears a smile ear to ear. Robin pulls Billy's face up for a kiss and they begin to dry hump in anticipation of coitus.

"I think that you made me squirt. I want your cock. Get that special goodie of yours out of these pants and get it inside of me."

Billy goes to take his pants off and feels warm liquid on his crotch.

"Take your pants off now!" Robin demands, which Billy finds to be far better and hotter than her actually ripping them off. Billy stands up, unzips his pants and once again feels a warm liquid on them. Billy looks at his hand and sees red. He wonders if his penis got caught and cut up on the zipper. Billy then looks at the white sheet between Robin's spread legs and sees a puddle of blood the size of a football.

"My God! Are you okay?"

"I'm fine. Just get your cock inside me already."

"No. No. Seriously, are you okay?" Billy points to between her legs, "There's blood!"

Robin looks down and shrieks, "My new sheets!"

"What about your pussy?"

"Holy shit! That's from me?"

Robin bolts from her bedroom and races to her bathroom. Billy sits on the bed next to the puddle of blood and wonders if there are arteries inside of a vagina and hopes that he didn't accidentally burst an artery inside of Robin. His lack of knowledge of this matter makes him wish that he had paid more attention in sex education and anatomy classes. What if Robin dies in the bathroom? The cops are never going to believe that Billy has accidentally fingerbanged Robin to death. He begins to panic. Billy is staring at the blood and wishing for it to not be there. The wait for Robin feels like an eternity. After five minutes, Billy wonders if Robin really is dead. He remembers reading that a human being can bleed to death in less than five minutes if an artery is severed. Billy wishes that he knew where all of the arteries are on a woman and then realizes that not knowing where all of the arteries on a woman are just adds to the complexity of women and his own complete lack of understanding of them.

After an excruciating seven more minutes Robin finally comes back into her bedroom. She's walking with a towel wrapped around her hips and is holding her crotch. Robin informs Billy that she isn't bleeding anymore but that she must have been bleeding when she climaxed.

"How many fingers did you have inside of me?"

Billy points to his wrist, "You had me up to here."

"In the future we need to be more careful when we want to fuck one another after a couple of glasses of wine."

"Agreed."

Billy and Robin sit on her bed in silence for several minutes. The playful sexual spirits that were in the air all day around them are gone. The sizeable amount of blood that came out of Robin's vagina killed any chance of Billy getting laid tonight. Robin puts on some underwear. Billy takes this as a cue to get dressed and leave. They quietly kiss at the door. As Billy walks to the elevator he hears the sound of Robin locking the deadbolt and the chain. He feels defeated.

Chapter 23

It's Friday morning. This is Billy's last day of work before he needs to check into the bank's alcohol dependency program in upstate New York on Tuesday. Billy isn't working on Monday so that his colleagues and sister might actually believe that he is working in the bank's San Francisco office for the month. Billy has come to work mostly sober and has been on time each day since the drug test. Despite playing with fire, Billy has successfully kept himself out of trouble all week by way of dumb luck. He knows that his life has been in a tailspin ever since he fell off of the wagon eight months ago when he first met Mia. He knows that he needs to stop drinking but he isn't sure if he is ready to give it up again. Each taste of alcohol feels like the breath of freedom for a man who has finally escaped after a lifetime in prison. Chris stops at Billy's desk on his usual morning head count.

"Morning, Bill."

"Good morning, Chris."

"I'm leaving early today to head out to my beach house and simply want to wish you luck over the upcoming weeks. I know that it will be tough but it will be worth it. I look forward to you coming back better and stronger in mind, body and spirit."

"Thank you, Chris."

Chris carefully places his left hand awkwardly onto Billy's shoulder. "No. Thank you, Bill." Chris then walks away.

"Condescending prick." Billy says under his breath as Chris continues along on his morning head count.

Shortly past four, after completing an honest day of work, Billy clears and locks his desk for the foreseeable future. He then goes to Robin's desk to see how she is feeling today. Robin isn't at her desk so Billy asks Jackie when Robin will be back.

"Robin didn't come in today."

Billy's eyes open wide at the news. He assumes that Robin died overnight from her vaginal wound and assumes that the police are on their way to the office right now and that they will have a hard time believing that Robin was enjoying having so much of his hand inside of her. He then wonders if confessing to all of the bank robberies will somehow help get him off of a murder charge. He knows that either way he'll be doing some serious time. He just doesn't want to be seen as a murderer.

"Did she say what's wrong?"

"She said that she has gonorrhea and that her doctor told her that it's the worst case that he's seen in over 30 years of practicing medicine." Jackie whispers.

Billy's face drops. "What?"

"Gonorrhea, it's an STD. Have you ever had it?"

"No."

"From what I hear it burns like an intense fire so much so that it makes a man's penis feel like it is simultaneously burning and being eaten alive by fire ants."

"Really." Billy's mouth suddenly dries out and his face turns pale.

Jackie laughs, "I'm kidding. Robin called out sick and told me that you somehow managed to break her vagina last night. She needs a day to rest off whatever it is that you did with her."

"Oh. Well. That's good. That's good. Let her know that I wish her well with that."

"Yeah, it looks like Robin isn't as strong as I am. I nearly broke you in half and I'll gladly do it again."

"Jackie. I have to go."

Billy is frightened at the prospect of being manhandled by Jackie again and needs a drink to calm his nerves. Billy heads over to the Farm to see if Mia is there. Billy figures that if Mia is there he can kill two birds with one stone in that he can get drunk and check in to see how Mia is doing.

The Farm still has its daytime lights on when Billy enters. The floors are freshly clean and the scent of bleach is still lingering in the air. Billy always finds bars to be the most depressing when they are brightly lit. With the lights on he can see the cheap wood of the bar and the haggard faces of the people within the establishment. A couple of old men who are daytime drunks are at the bar giving their elbows a workout with Basil behind the bar.

"What are you doing here, Billy?"

"I'm stopping by to see if I could get a few drinks and to see if Mia is around. I'm worried about her."

"She's not working today and you didn't seem too worried about her the other night when she was a crying mess."

"That's a long story that should remain between Mia and myself."

"Alright. Fair enough. I invented a new drink. It's called Broken Sunglasses because when someone drinks them until the sun comes up they'll fall down and break the sunglasses on their face. It's good."

"I'll try it."

Billy drinks several Broken Sunglasses. Each one tastes stronger than the previous one. At one in the morning Billy realizes that he has had enough and should head home. Billy wishes Basil well and tells him that won't be around for a few weeks since he will be going out to San Francisco for work. Billy leaves the bar and wonders what compelled him to lie to Basil about San Francisco. Basil couldn't care less about Billy's work life. The night air is warm and the streets are relatively empty for New York standards. Most everyone is away at the beaches for the weekend.   Billy is heading towards the Broadway-Lafayette subway station but doesn't get far. Two bars down from the Farm, Billy runs into an old drinking buddy of his, Ronnie, who he hasn't seen since he had to use a fake ID to enter bars.

"Billy!"

They instantly recognize one another in their own drunken haze and talk outside of the bar for a few minutes. Ronnie has been taking in the night air with an older man who is smoking a cigarette.

"Come on in for a beer," Ronnie insists.

"I'm broke."

"I'm paying," An older man says before introducing himself as a retired commodities trader who just met Ronnie while they were both drinking alone at the bar. Billy doesn't remember much about Ronnie, except for his face, the fact that Ronnie is a couple of years older than Billy and that Ronnie was a decent college football player who never realized his dream of the NFL. They enter the mostly empty establishment and grab stools at the bar.

"Show him the game," Ronnie tells the older man, who then takes a coaster to the edge of the bar, flips it up in the air, and catches it in one swift motion. "We're trying to see who can do the most."

"I'm game."

Billy finds the flip the coaster game to be more fun than he ever could have imagined. Ronnie holds the record with seven coasters. As Billy flips the coasters, he has multiple shots and two beers. His attempt to get home after an evening of drinking is dashed. Billy is now a stumbling drunk and tells Ronnie that it was good to run into him. Billy thanks the older man for introducing him to the coaster flip game and for treating him to the drinks. Billy finally continues along his way to the subway. In his drunken stupor Billy decides that it will be a good idea to call Chris' voicemail up at the bank and leave him a message in his Cleary McLennon voice. Cleary McLennon is a voice that Billy does at the bank to crack up his coworkers. It is the voice of a fictitious old Irish man who also happens to be the grandfather of one of Billy's coworkers. The voice cracks people up at the bank.

"This is Cleary McLennon! Just calling to say hellloooo! And see how my granddaughter Emily is doing!!! Chickety cha! Chickety cha! Cha! Cha! Cha! Chickety Cha!" Billy blurts into Chris' voicemail before hanging up to walk down the steps to the subway.

Chapter 24

It is half past noon. The hot sun shines through Billy's open blinds and smacks him in the face as he snores from being asleep on his back. The hum of the air conditioning is creating enough white noise for Billy to sleep through the morning sun. He exhales an extremely long breath of air and begins to choke on his own snore as he inhales. The choking wakes Billy up. He lifts his head to look at the time and feels the massive headache of a hangover and moans. This is Billy's first ever hangover. Billy knows that he shouldn't have allowed himself to have gotten so drunk last night but he also knows that he has never really been able to stop drinking once he has started. Liquor is too readily available for Billy. However, the last thing that he wants to do today is drink. The thought of drinking is making Billy feel the need to dry heave. Nothing comes out, so Billy feeds his cats and heads to the shower.

Only the cold water is turned on as Billy steps inside the shower and cries. The feeling of a hangover is new to him and causes tears to fall down his face. The water feels frigid. Billy gasps for air in the cold as he goes back and forth beneath the running water. He ponders his last few days of freedom before going to treatment on Tuesday. The shower lasts under three minutes. It's Billy's go to trick for getting up and out of the house quickly. A cold shower makes it impossible to stay stuck in one's own thoughts for too long and forces the necessary bathing to continue unabated.

Billy is clean. His eyes have stopped tearing. He dries himself off, gets dressed and pours himself both a glass of milk and a glass of orange juice. He takes turns sipping from each glass. Billy has heard that a combination of both milk and orange juice help hangovers go away quickly. Though Billy realizes that the milk and orange juice might only be psychosomatic he continues with this voodoo-like hangover cure since the act of drinking the milk and juice might do something for his brain and make it stop hurting. Billy opens his window and sticks his head out. He sees the sun brightly shining down on him. Only a few small clouds are high up in the sky. The heat and humidity hit him on the face. It feels as though it is going to be an extra hot day. It feels like the sort of day that Billy would normally stay indoors with his air conditioning on but since he has only a few days on freedom left he figures that he should check out the lay of the land before his 30 day confinement.

Billy leaves his apartment and heads to the subway. By the time he reaches the station he is a sweaty mess. He goes down the steps to the R train and smells the terrible scent of urine and feces thanks to his station being one that has several middle aged homeless men who are fall down drunks living inside of it at the end of the platform. Billy steps onto the train a split second before the doors close and pulls out of the station. The air conditioning and better air quality feel good in Billy's lungs. At 9th Street Billy steps off the train and runs up several flights of stairs to transfer to an F train. He reaches the upper platform just in time to see the red lights on the back of a train pulling out at the end of the station and has to wait ten minutes in the heat for another train. Billy pats his head with a handkerchief to keep himself from visually being a sweaty mess until the next train comes. At Carroll Street, Billy exits the F train and is amazed at how cool this particular station is naturally before going up the stairs and exiting the subway system entirely.

Billy walks west down towards Pier 6 along Buttermilk Channel. A ferry is boarding at the dock when Billy gets within eyesight. Billy races to the boat so that he will not have to wait 30 minutes for the next one and is one of the last stragglers allowed onboard before the ferry pulls off and away from the dock. Billy takes a seat on the open upper deck of the ferry and is on the receiving end of a warm breeze that is full of diesel exhaust from the boat. Billy stays on the upper deck despite the fumes from the exhaust going straight into his lungs because he has an unnecessary fear of getting trapped inside the lower level of the boat and drowning. The ferry docks at Governors Island six minutes after departing Brooklyn. Billy disembarks and is greeted to the island by a man in a blue shirt speaking into a bullhorn. "Welcome to Governors Island. Ferry service runs to and from Manhattan every 30 minutes on the hour and the half hour."

As Billy walks off the dock and onto the island he feels a sense of relief. Governors Island has always been a place where Billy feels safe and at home despite it being a public park. The island is spotted with open fields and old forts. Billy's love of forts is just below his love of booze, money, and women. The added bonus for Billy is that the island is stacked with beautiful young single women who are yearning to be there with a man of their dreams. They're hoping to have the Manhattan skyline as a backdrop to a first kiss that makes them feel as though they are living in a real life movie. Billy knows that the mystique of Governors Island is an easy panty dropper.

Before heading to the old fort, Billy goes west to the interior part of the island where a food court comprised of food trucks and small shacks is set up. Billy orders a pulled pork sandwich and scarfs it down. Now the only thing standing between Billy and the end of his hangover is time. With a stomach full of food, Billy heads to the northern section of the island that has an old fort overlooking lower Manhattan. It is the location that has the best view of Manhattan from Governors Island and is known to Billy as an easy pick up location. Billy takes a seat on the lawn up against the fort and waits for the perfect opportunity to begin a conversation with a lady. Several beautiful ladies stand between Billy and the water. They take self portraits with Manhattan's skyline behind them. Though they are all pretty in their own way, so far none of them has the spark that catches Billy's full attention. Billy's phone rings. It's Mia.

"Hello?"

"Billy?"

"Yes, Mia."

"Hey, um... I was wondering if you already had plans for your birthday. It's tomorrow, right?"

"Yes, it is tomorrow and I don't have any plans for it."

"You don't? Good. Can I take you to the aquarium out in Coney Island?"

"I haven't been to the aquarium in years. I'd love to go there with you for my birthday."

"Perfect! Can I meet you there at one?"

"Sure thing."

"Great. See you there."

They hang up and Billy spots his mark. She's a beautiful woman in her 20s, with short black hair, tattoos on her right shoulder and she is wearing a white sleeveless top with black jeans. The red lipstick and black eyeliner scream "GIVE ME YOUR FULL ATTENTION, I'M SINGLE!" This young beauty keeps taking self portrait after self portrait at the fence by the water in front of Billy. She keeps looking at each photo and then takes another because she seems unhappy with the result of each one. Billy jumps up at the opportunity to help her.

"Excuse me, would you like for me to take a few photos for you?"

"Absolutely, I've been trying to get the perfect shot."

She hands Billy her cell phone to snap photos, heads back to the fence, and gives the camera a pose that she couldn't have done while holding the cell phone herself. She smiles, throws one hand up and the other out and down in a ta-da sort of way. Her smile makes her beam with beauty. Billy snaps away.

"I think some of these might be good. Take a look."

"I love these."

"Good to hear. My name is Billy."

Billy extends his right hand as the beautiful woman extends hers.

"Billy, I'm Annabelle and it's a pleasure."

Billy lifts Annabelle's hand and gives it a soft quick peck of a kiss. It's a cheesy move but it works. This whole scene that Billy has carefully orchestrated and laid in wait for is working like a charm. Billy has done the same introduction after snapping a few photos for beautiful women a half a dozen times in the same location over the past two years. Annabelle is from the Midwest and is hooked instantly by Billy's bait of living a New York fairytale straight out of a movie. Being found and helped by a handsome stranger in the middle of what she suspects is a dangerous New York is what Annabelle has hoped for since moving to the city six months ago.

Billy and Annabelle stroll through Governors Island, laughing, and snap more photos of each other. At times, Billy offers Annabelle his arm, which she happily takes, wrapping her arm around his.

Annabelle cannot believe the amount of luck that she has run into today by meeting Billy. They eventually take a seat on the grass below a large London plane tree where they have their first kiss in the heat and humidity as the sound of water from New York Harbor crashing up against the sea wall. Annabelle thinks that she has found her prince charming and Billy thinks that he has found his next one night stand. They stay beneath the shade of the tree and make out and caress one another in the literal same spot that Billy has kissed a half dozen other beautiful young women. Annabelle tells Billy how funny her apartment is because she doesn't have any blinds hanging on the windows and that her blinds have been sitting in the corner of her bedroom since she moved in just waiting to be hung.   She can't reach the top of the window to hang them. Billy tells Annabelle that he can hang them for her sometime knowing full well that Annabelle will jump at the opportunity for her prince charming to hang the blinds for her. Annabelle then asks Billy to come back to her apartment and they take the next ferry to Manhattan.

Annabelle's apartment is on the 27th floor of a high rise on Reade Street in Tribeca. It is a doorman building with a concierge service that could have easily been used to help hang the blinds but Annabelle didn't use them because she knew that she was going to meet her prince charming and that he would hang them for her. Annabelle has an electric drill and a screwdriver attachment. Billy has hung many blinds in various apartments scattered throughout New York City. He's grown so accustomed to hanging blinds that he hangs seven sets for Annabelle in less than 20 minutes. Annabelle's New York dream, the one that she has thought about since her days in junior high is coming true before her eyes.

"Billy, you hung my blinds. You're my hero."

"It was nothing."

"No, it means a lot. You don't understand. I have had to walk around in a towel whenever I got out of the shower to pick out clothes because I don't want the neighbors to see me naked. You're my hero."

"Really, you think so?" Billy asks her, as he looks out the window and sees that her neighbors are people in offices a thousand feet away.

"I sure do."

Annabelle kisses Billy and leads him forward towards her as she walks backwards to allow herself to fall back onto her bed and have Billy fall on top of her. Twenty minutes later, Annabelle is begging Billy to spend the night with her as he tries his best to leave her apartment sans tears, sans the realization that she was just used for sex that lasted a mere 30 seconds. She is under the impression that she has met the man of her dreams today. She's already thinking about what sort of white dress to wear at their wedding and is wondering what Billy's last name is to see if she will want to hyphenate it or take it on altogether. Billy kisses Annabelle goodnight and has no intention of ever seeing her again. There will never be an Annabelle Hansen or Annabelle Carver-Hansen.

Chapter 25

Billy exits the subway at the end of the line in Coney Island. It's an even hotter and more humid afternoon than the day before. There are lines of people crowding around Nathan's for hot dogs. Billy develops a mustache of sweat as he walks along Surf Avenue and passing the many amusement park rides. He stops to admire both the Cyclone and the Wonder Wheel. He's terrified of both but can work through his fear of the Cyclone to ride it once a year. The rust on the near century-old steel of the Wonder Wheel makes the ride too scary for Billy to ever ride even though he finds the colorful paint scheme on it to be a majestic sight. As Billy nears the aquarium he can see that Mia is off in the distance waiting for him. Mia looks beautiful despite having a terrible sadness in her eyes. Mia gives Billy a half smile and a short "hey." Billy's heart races with anxious feelings. There are several awkward pauses between them because they do not know what to do or say. The last time they saw one another Mia had confessed that she wanted to do speed every day and Billy sort of ended their relationship.

"Can we go for a walk?"

"Sure."

They walk over to the beach and down near the water, close to where waves crash onto the shore. Tiny bits of salty water crash up into the air and land on them.

"I had no idea that you felt that way and so strongly about drug use. If I had known, I never would have done speed again."

"I didn't think that I could tell you about my feelings on drugs because I needed to let you do your own thing. I didn't want you to be sneaky about drug use or cause you to hide any sort of habit from me."

"I don't ever want to do speed or any other drug again. I threw out the rest of what I had bought. You mean too much to me for me to do that stuff ever again. Billy, I love you."

"I love you too, Mia."

Billy and Mia hug as tears run silently down Billy's face.

"I'm serious. I'm never going to do speed or anything else again."

"That sounds like a good plan that you have."

Despite the tears on his face, Billy is still keeping his emotions guarded, at least verbally, and doesn't even truly know how to verbalize his feelings to Mia about the situation.

"Will you please take me back if I promise to never ever take drugs again? Seriously, I'm done doing drugs." Mia says, with her fingers crossed behind Billy's back.

"Please don't ever do drugs again. I've seen drugs do lots of bad things to people and I love you too much to stick around and watch you destroy yourself."

Billy and Mia pause, standing with their arms around one another's waist and looking into one another's eyes. Billy cannot help but see that Mia's light brown eyes are picking up all of the light beautifully, while Mia can see that Billy's eyes are red and bloodshot.

"So, will you take me back?" Mia asks with her eyebrows raised, giving Billy a sad puppy dog face.

"I didn't know that we officially broke up. You ran off before I could finish what I was saying."

"I knew what you were going to say and I couldn't stand to hear it." Mia says with a smile.

"Of course I'll take you back."

"Perfect. But I just want to let you know that I think that we should take things slowly this time and not rush into things."

"That sounds like it will be a good thing."

As they walk hand in hand towards the aquarium Mia takes two tickets for the aquarium out of her purse and hands one to Billy.

"Happy Birthday!" Mia says, as her big smile beams rays of goodness into Billy's bloodshot eyes causing Billy to smile.

Billy and Mia enter the aquarium. They slowly walk through each exhibit and make sure to spot each and every last fish that is listed on all of the tanks. While walking between exhibits, Mia offers Billy one of her patented piggy back rides. Billy hops on Mia's back. Mia happily begins carrying Billy to the next exhibit but suddenly drops him off of her back after a few short steps.

"Oh my God! I felt your penis poking me in my back. That's disgusting."

"Sorry, I really can't control it with you." Billy tells her sheepishly.

Mia is still annoyed at Billy for getting aroused in his pants from her touch, even after his apology. A literal and figurative black cloud grows above their heads as they walk into the seal show without discussing Billy's boner any further. The heavens open up as they sit watching seals clap and wave to the crowd in exchange for small fish treats. It pours as if Noah should have begun building an ark. The abrupt rainfall causes an early end to their afternoon at the aquarium. Neither Billy nor Mia have an umbrella and are soaked to the bone by the time they walk past the Cyclone towards the N train. The rain stops as suddenly as it began when Billy and Mia get a mere 20 or so feet from the shelter of the subway entrance. Billy and Mia are soaked to the bone and are now laughing at how drenched the other is.

While heading back to Billy's apartment the air conditioning of the subway feels downright frigid on their wet bodies. Billy and Mia cannot wait to dry off and warm up.

Billy opens his apartment door and goes straight into his bedroom to change into dry clothes while Mia goes into the bathroom and tries to dry off her wet clothing with a hairdryer. As Billy pulls dry clothes out of his dresser drawers he gets what he thinks is a brilliant idea. He walks naked into the kitchen, locates the whipped cream in his refrigerator and sprays some onto himself.

Mia walks out of the bathroom and finds Billy in his birthday suit with whipped cream strategically covering his fluffed penis. The visual of Billy looking like a poor excuse of a male stripper makes Mia burst out into uncontrollable laughter. She tells Billy that they can't fool around anymore because they need to go slowly this time around and that they need to be the type of friends who don't see each other naked or have sex at first. Billy is stunned by this news.

Earlier in the day Billy thought that take things slowly meant something else entirely; like maybe they shouldn't have unprotected sex with one another to avoid pregnancy scares. Billy asks Mia if she is sure that she doesn't want to lick the now melting whipped cream off of him. Mia dries tears of laughter from her face and is positive that she wants no part of Billy or the whipped cream. Billy walks into the bathroom, sticks his manhood into his sink and washes it off with cold water while feeling sullen.

Instead of having birthday sex, Billy and Mia watch the Sound of Music for the millionth time. Mia chooses to not spend the night with Billy, so he walks her to the subway. They say goodbye to one another with a big hug and kisses on the cheek at the turnstile gate of the 93rd Street entrance. Billy swipes Mia through the turnstile with his MetroCard. She heads towards the stairs to go down to the platform where the trains are as Billy heads back towards the stairs that head up to the street. When Billy gets to the base of the steps he turns back around. He wants to see Mia one last time and upon turning sees that Mia has turned around too to look back at him at the exact same moment. Billy and Mia smile their last genuine smile to one another before heading their separate ways knowing full well that neither of them will see the other ever again. This is their last time saying their last goodbye. Their love will be kept in time capsules in their memory banks and will be remembered as being much better than it ever really was. Billy returns to his apartment. He needs to ready his man-purse for the robbery as Mia takes the subway to her coworker's apartment and buys herself another bag of speed.

Chapter 26

The weather report on the morning news is that it will be another scorcher of a day with a high of 95 degrees and 100% humidity. It's the type of day that makes Billy wonder why he still lives in New York. The tourists will be getting their money's worth with the smell of New York on this day. Billy turns off the weather report as his air conditioner blows a steady 67 degrees. Billy does one last double check of his man-purse to see that he has everything before walking over to a local car service. Billy gets into the back of an old beat up black town car which smells of bad cologne and has the flair of a carnival sideshow curtain. The car speeds Billy to his destination with the cab driver swiftly pulling up to the curb at 36th Street and 4th Avenue anxious to get his next fare. Billy walks down to the subway, he knows from the photos released by the police department that the security cameras at this subway station are old and grainy. They are of no use in identifying anyone. The token booth clerk is an older man who looks like a defeated hippie. Billy uses small bills to buy himself a new MetroCard with cash at the booth. He does this so that the cash that he uses will be handed out in change and the transaction will be untraceable back to him. Billy swipes through the turnstile and goes down to the platform. The platform is full of stuffy hot air which causes Billy's clothes stick to his skin. After waiting several minutes Billy feels a rush of cool air move across the platform as the train approaches and pulls into the station. The subway car that stops in front of Billy is empty. It's a telltale sign that something is wrong with the car. The doors open and Billy gags at the terrible smell that emanates from this particular subway car. The awful scent is being directly caused by odors wafting up and off of a homeless man. Billy runs over to the next car for fresher air. This subway car is crowded with people who have all fled the stench. At the next station Billy runs again to the next subway car. This third car is less crowded and Billy takes a seat. He carefully begins to cover each of his fingertips with bandages until all are neatly covered and no trace of a fingerprint can be left. When the train reaches the East River, Billy is the only person left inside of this particular subway car. As he passes over the river, Billy carefully puts on his prosthetic face. By the time the train stops at Canal Street Billy has transformed himself and is completely unrecognizable with his prosthetics, sunglasses, and hat. Billy exits the subway at 23rd Street and walks down to the coffee shop that is across from Derico's apartment on Park Avenue.

It's a little after one in the afternoon as Billy enters the coffee shop and scans it for undercover cops. He takes a seat at the window and looks out onto the street. From this seat Billy waits for Derico and continues to be on the lookout for cops. Billy looks for people wearing bulky bulletproof vests and people carrying a police radio and for people and cars that keep circling the street without any purpose or direction. If Billy's internal cop antenna goes off he will be forced to call off and abandon the robbery.

At 1:30, Derico exits his apartment and walks towards the bank. Dark storm clouds begin to roll in over his head. Billy hopes that the rain will hold off until after the robbery. He watches in disbelief at the clockwork with which Derico does his banking business. He casually gets up and exits the coffee shop so that he can follow Derico into the bank. Billy then hurries across the street. He needs to get himself into the proper position on the commercial banking line inside the bank so that he will be able to easily take Derico's deposit.

As Billy enters the bank he is hit with a strong scent of air freshener mixed with cheap cologne. Frank Derico is the next customer on the line to see the commercial teller. Mandi Whalen is behind the bulletproof glass. She hands stacks of singles and fives to a man who needs the small denominations to give out as change in his small convenience store. Billy stands in line directly behind

Derico and learns that Derico has doused himself with too much cologne today. Derico is clueless as to what Billy is about to do and that the man whom he caught following him a couple of weeks ago is now standing behind him. Derico is holding his deposit today in a small black leather bag that has a zipper and a clasp lock on it in his right hand. Derico's man-purse is European and puts Billy's no name man-purse to shame. Billy waits patiently as Mandi counts Derico's deposit. While Derico walks to the front door of the bank looking down at his deposit slip Mandi smiles and says "next" to Billy. Billy steps forward smiling with a closed mouth and presses his note up to the glass.

BANK ROBBERY. MANDI WHALEN I KNOW WHERE YOU LIVE. GIVE ME THE LAST FOUR CASH DEPOSITS OR I WILL FIND YOU IN THE MIDDLE OF THE NIGHT.

Mandi begins to grab the cash from her drawer that hasn't just been deposited. Billy notices that Mandi's hand is coming from the wrong side of the drawer. Mandi is trying to give Billy marked cash with either a dye pack or a GPS transmitter inside of it. Billy taps on the glass and gestures to the bottom of his note.

"YOUR HOUSE MATEY!" Billy boasts in a terrible attempt at an Australian accent.

Mandi puts the marked bills back into her drawer and slides the last four cash deposits through the small opening at the bottom of the bulletproof glass. Billy places the cash inside of his man-purse and calmly walks toward the door. Billy's back is to the tellers and he has no idea that Mandi has unlocked herself from behind the safety of the bulletproof glass and is now following him. As Billy walks through the door and out onto the street Mandi takes several packs of singles and throws them at him through the open door and out onto the street. The packs of singles explode when they are ten feet away from the bank's door. They create a cloud of smoke as ink is sent in every direction. Billy flinches and jumps at the explosion of the bills and then looks back and sees Mandi coming towards him. Billy is in shock. The left side of his face and his clothes are covered in ink.

"Don't fuck with me, prick!" Mandi shouts with a thick Brooklyn accent that only comes out when she's angry, just like Billy's.

Mandi continues walking towards Billy and has the look of murderous rage on her face. Billy is irate and mad as hell too but knows that he can't fight Mandi because he will certainly get caught if he stays around. The silent alarm was triggered more than 45 seconds ago and the police dispatchers are now putting word of the robbery out on the airwaves. Billy begins to run west on 23rd Street with Mandi following directly behind him.

"Hey, don't run. Asshole. You're dead."

Billy hears Mandi's words behind him. He is terrified about getting caught and turns his speed up a notch. He tries to wipe the ink from his face while running which only causes more of his face to become covered in ink. A crowd of people are walking slowly towards Billy and are rudely taking up the entire sidewalk. Billy cannot get around them so he throws up his elbows and smashes through the middle of the crowd. Billy hits several of the people as he barrels through the crowd and causes two of the pedestrians to get knocked down to the pavement. The crowd does nothing to slow Mandi as she jumps over them as though she is an Olympic hurdler.

Madison Square Park is across the street. It will most definitely have an undercover cop or two inside of it while a police precinct is a couple of blocks to the south. Billy's best route of escape is to run north alongside the park. Lightning flashes and thunder crashes. Hail and a heavy rain begin to fall. Mandi continues to follow. It is clear to Billy that Mandi wants Billy's blood for making the threats against her. Despite all of Billy's reconnaissance for this bank robbery he doesn't know that Mandi Whalen's maiden name is Montalbano, let alone the fact that she is the daughter of a hitman, who regularly works for the Italian mafia. The only thing about Mandi Whalen that Billy is aware of is that she is one tough woman. She is much tougher than the aura that she gives off on first glance. Billy knows that he will have to confront Mandi in order to get her to stop.

The sound of police sirens are in the air and are getting closer. Billy reaches inside of his man-purse and pulls out one of the burner cell phones that he always keeps inside of a zipper compartment in case of emergency. The phones were paid for in cash and are untraceable back to Billy. He hopes that the rain won't kill the phone as he dials 911. He reports that he is in an office building on 49th Street and Park Avenue and that there is a guy with guns who has shot several of his coworkers. Billy is out of breath from running, so this tricks the 911 operator into believing that this isn't a prank call. Billy tells the operator that he needs to hang up so that he can go hide in a quiet place until the cops can come rescue him. He hangs up the phone and throws it away. He's drenched and feels like his face is getting welts from the hail hitting it. Billy reaches into his bag and pulls out a second burner phone and calls 911 again. This time he reports that there are bombs in five different public schools. One in each borough and that they are set to blow up at two o'clock sharp. Billy hangs up, turns back and throws the phone at Mandi, hitting her in the left shoulder with it. Billy's bogus 911 calls do several things: they divert the bank robbery response to the active shooter, they cause police to go to hundreds of public schools throughout the city, and best of all, the bogus calls cause the streets to flood with more than a million school children and teachers all at once. The crowds will allow Billy to hide in plain sight. Billy just needs to get rid of the beast that is Mandi who is continuing to follow him.

As Billy approaches the northern portion of the park he notices that the police sirens begin to get further away and fade off into the distance. Billy is in the clear from a uniformed response to his escape and can now turn his attention to eliminating the threat of capture that Mandi is still creating. Billy turns left and stops at the north side of the park. When Mandi turns the corner, Billy pounces at her, hitting her with his shoulder and knocking her to the sidewalk. Billy then grabs Mandi in a most violent way.

"Stop following me. You need to stop following me."

"You're a dead man." Mandi says, and spits into Billy's face before continuing, "My father's going to find you and chop you into pieces. They will never find all the pieces of your body, let alone be able to put you back together."

"STOP FOLLOWING ME!" Billy yells, as he puts all of his weight onto Mandi's right leg, twisting it at the knee, until he hears and feels the knee dislocate in a most gruesome manner. The pain of a dislocated knee causes Mandi to let out a scream of death. She reaches up and scratches Billy's neck with her fingernails in one final attempt to stop him. Billy runs off into a crowd of people who are walking in the rainstorm with ponchos on before catching the lone available taxi heading south along Broadway as the streets begin to flood with schoolchildren.

The robbery went horribly wrong and Billy knows this. Aside from the man-purse being full of money everything else is fucked up beyond all belief. Billy is a sweaty mess who is struggling to catch his breath and has a large amount of ink on his face and body from the dye pack explosions. Billy is in disbelief at how wrong everything went and is shocked that he had to resort to violence. The streets are now packed wall to wall with people from all of the schools being evacuated. Traffic is moving at a snail's pace from the crowds and rain as Billy sits low in the backseat of the taxi. His stomach and hands are now trembling uncontrollably.

"Stop the cab."

Billy opens the door and vomits out of the taxi while in the middle of Broadway as other taxis honk their horn at Billy for creating a further bottleneck. Billy feels better for having emptied his stomach and closes the door. The cab continues south and then heads over the Brooklyn Bridge as Billy's stomach weakens again. Billy struggles to maintain some form of composure. His stomach and hands are still shaking uncontrollably from the fear as the fast moving storm clears. Billy knows that he can't do his usual routines of using the taxi as a getaway to the subway, or using a taxi before nonchalantly walking home. The ink covering him will alert too many people to what he did today. Billy has to think quickly. Instead of stopping off at 65th Street and 4th Avenue Billy has the cab continue further down into Bay Ridge and has the cab driver let him out a block away from Bliss Park.

As Billy steps out of the taxi and into the sun, he finds the heat and humidity to be unbearable once again. The mustache of sweat happens again in an instant. Billy walks towards Bliss Park while shaking and feeling terrified and paranoid. He keeps looking over his shoulder as he attempts to walk calmly towards Bliss Park. He feels as though someone must have followed him but can't seem to notice anyone following him. He figures that they must be experts at blending in. Billy zigzags through the spacious park so as to avoid close contact with the few people who are in the park. He cannot let anyone see the ink on his face or his clothing up close. He walks up the footpaths to the top of the hill that overlooks the Narrows of New York harbor. He takes a deep breath as he takes one last look over his shoulder and then walks down into the brush and thicket that grows along the side of the hill facing the water. Billy lays down in the shade, making himself as flat as he can get so that he is hidden in the thicket. He is scared out of his mind and thirsty as can be but he is without water. Billy waits for night to fall and only has his terrified thoughts to keep him company. Billy realizes that his life has quickly spun out of control and that he needs help. Aside from getting caught by the police Billy cannot imagine his life getting any worse than it already is now.

Billy lays and listens to his terrified paranoid thoughts and the hum of the Belt Parkway in the background beneath him. Billy listens to the birds chirp in the trees and sees a large hawk circling overheard. It's eyeballing him through the thicket with wonder about whether or not Billy can be a meal. By the time Billy finally calms himself down he wonders whether or not it is ironic to be having such strange terrified and paranoid thoughts while hiding out in a place called Bliss Park. He's unsure about the exact definition of irony and tends to assume that he always has a complete misunderstanding as to what irony is.

As the sun sets Billy's mind can taste freedom. Once it is completely dark outside, Billy walks along the desolate bike path, which runs parallel to the Narrows between the water and the Belt Parkway. The darkness combined with the lights coming off of the cars on the Belt Parkway makes it impossible for passersby to see the ink that Billy is covered in.   Billy takes a foot bridge over the Belt Parkway and then walks along the quiet tree-lined back streets of Bay Ridge towards his apartment. When Billy finally enters his apartment he rips off his prosthetics and jumps into the shower with a bottle of vodka. Billy washes the ink and sweat off of himself by using a bar of Lava soap while simultaneously downing the vodka on an empty stomach. In the last moment before blacking out Billy has the realization that he should finally look up the definition of irony in the dictionary. He feels as though he has probably experienced it somewhere in life. He simply isn't sure where it may have been.

The author would like to thank his wife Kristen, Janice Erlbaum, Lori Mocha, Evan Apostolakos, Laura Melia Kelly and Barry Sobel.

www.ingramcontent.com/pod-product-compliance
Lightning Source LLC
Chambersburg PA
CBHW060332260626
47160CB00007B/2779